ii

A Christian Fiction Novel

PRISCILLA

Subtitle

PAPER DOLLS

Author

Kara R. Hunt

ISBN: 978-1-959788-56-0

DEDICATION

Dedicated to the One Who paid the price for it all, so I wouldn't have to.

WHAT READERS ARE SAYING

Finding a woman who couldn't relate to any of the themes in Kara R Hunt's expertly crafted novel, Paper Dolls, would be difficult. Wife, mother, daughter, sibling, friend, females struggling with identity, hope, hopelessness, dreams, and dreaded decisions. The intricate plot is a layer-upon-layer of deep emotional entwinement paired with strong Christian values.

Hunt's writing is superb. These characters portray the author's attention to emotion, motivation, repressing and expressing old trauma, broken dreams, and the deepest, most horrifying fears, making them anything but paper cutouts of people. They are flesh and blood come to life in a memorable, extremely gifted, beautifully crafted story.

Dr. Deborah Maxey
Multi-award-winning author of The Endllng, A novel
Licensed Counselor and Marriage and Family Therapist

Paper Dolls, is for those who love Christian fiction about real people, who make real mistakes.

– Cheri Swalwell, Author and Speaker with Jesus in the Everyday

I really enjoyed following the lives of the women in Habakkuk - there's suspense, danger, mystery, and grace, all woven together in a beautiful story. Fans of Christian and women's fiction will love the characters and takeaway message that God can handle all of our problems. Complete with fun friendships, very clean romance, and prayer warriors, I highly recommend Paper Dolls for women of all stages in their Christian growth.

– M. Liz Boyle, Author of Avalanche, Chased, and Ablaze

This was a great Christian Fiction read from Ms. Hunt. Fast-paced and rife with tension, this story had twists I didn't see coming, lock-tight friendships, complex relationships, and the added bonus of well-placed humor. I got attached to the characters and found myself rooting for them from the start. Mostly I enjoyed the thread of grace that ran through the story and touched each of the women. Looking forward to the next installment and to reading more from Ms. Hunt.

– Jericha Kingston, Author of Lily Bloom

Paper Dolls is a wonderful story of five women from different situations who overcome through the power of prayer, love, and friendship. Raw characters, wonderful writing, and a gripping storyline make Ms. Hunt one to watch for in women's fiction. I look forward to the other books in the series.

**–   Candice Sue Patterson, Multi-published
Author of Modern, Vintage Romances**

Paper Dolls is filled with all the things that make women's fiction fans sit up and take notice. Family intrigue, a touch of romance, the pain of loss, the joy of reunion, and uncertainty of life. Walk with these women as they sort out their lives, their families, and their relationships - or at least try.

– Pegg Thomas, Author and Multiple Award-Winning Novelist

I'm hooked on this series ... I read Book One in the Habakkuk series and I knew I had to read Kite's story. It didn't disappoint. I won't give away spoilers, but be prepared to go on another adventure with these ladies and their families! I love how the author reconnected me with the other members of the community that we met in Book One. There's the right amount of intrigue, warfare, and relationship challenges to keep the story exciting. And hang on, because just when you think you know what'll happen next, you don't! Great book from Kara R. Hunt.

– Amazon Reviewer

Another great book by Kara R. Hunt! Beloved characters from Paper Dolls return for another wild adventure. Full of intrigue and suspense, Kite is sure to hook readers to the Habbakuk series and have them anxiously anticipating more.

– Amazon Reviewer

In "Kite," the second book of Hunt's "Paper Dolls" series, the reader follows a newly married Kite through a tangled web of family intrigue and danger that will keep readers turning the pages! Most of the cast of "Paper Dolls" make appearances in this book, it's like revisiting old friends.

– Amazon Reviewer

ACKNOWLEDGEMENTS

To everyone who has purchased, read, reviewed, and supported Book 1 and Book 2 in this series. May Book 3 be a blessing to you as well.

A SPECIAL NOTE TO MY READERS

This book is a work of fiction. While the characters and the town of Habakkuk are works of fiction, the situations and circumstances they find themselves in are not.

The LORD God is my strength, and he will make my feet like hinds' feet, and he will make me to walk upon mine high places.

- Habakkuk 3:19 KJV

Chapter 1

Priscilla King nuzzled her face against the dark brown one next to her.

His height matched her five-foot-seven frame perfectly, though Barry had told her the muscular specimen's height wasn't measured the same way hers was. She smiled and ran a hand through the dark mane that rivaled hers in color.

"Barry, I don't know what to say. Except … I think I'm falling in love."

Barry thrust out his chest. "With me or with Rich Brown?"

Priscilla's heart raced. Not again. Not now. Not after she and Barry had spent the last three years enjoying their marriage and forgetting her past. She searched her memory for anyone with that name and came up blank. She looked at Barry and swallowed. "Rich Brown?"

He nodded.

Priscilla sucked in a breath and held it. After a few seconds, she asked, "Do I know him?"

He chuckled. "I hope so. He's standing right next to you."

Priscilla turned again to the beautiful animal standing next to her, and her muscles relaxed. His dark brown eyes looked at her as though she should've known who he was. "Are you Rich?"

The horse stared at her.

Barry sidled up next to her. "I didn't say his name was Rich. I said Rich Brown. Ask him if that's his name."

She looked into the almond-shaped eyes again. "Are you Rich Brown?"

The horse whinnied and tapped his right hoof on the ground twice.

Priscilla laughed and rubbed her nose against Rich Brown's. "Oh, Barry. Rich and I are going to get along just great."

Barry patted the horse's back. "Jim Voss, the previous owner and a friend of mine, said his wife named him that because of the richness of his dark brown coloring."

Priscilla walked around the horse and stopped to look at his tail, which was just as black as his mane. "What kind of horse is he?"

"A Missouri Fox Trotter. I have experience with this horse and breed. Jim knew that and asked if I'd consider buying him. I told him yes. I knew Rich Brown would be perfect for you."

"You've ridden him before?"

"Many times. Especially when Jim and I would take to the local trails. You've mentioned how you've always wanted to learn to ride and Rich Brown would be perfect for that. He's a good horse."

"He's beautiful."

Barry adjusted the black Stetson he wore when he worked with his horses. "Jim and his family were pretty attached, so it was an emotional sale. Jim asked me to buy Rich because he knew I'd take good care of him."

Priscilla narrowed her eyes. "If they were so attached, why did they put him up for sale?"

He sighed. "Jim's getting older and having some health issues. He thought handing the business side of things over to his son would relieve some of the stress." Barry kicked at the dirt. "It didn't."

"What do you mean?"

"Despite his son's degrees in business and accounting, he failed miserably at managing the family business. Now the Voss Horse Ranch is facing bankruptcy."

"That's awful."

"It is." He motioned to the other side of the fence. "So I purchased a couple more from him as well."

Priscilla leaned against the white rail fencing and looked at the two new horses that had been added to the pen. One was tall, gray, and had white covering the bottom of his hind legs, the other was light tan and speckled.

She'd discovered Barry's love of horses the first day he'd given her a tour of his estate. At first, she was terrified of the large animals and kept her distance, but he reached for her hand and walked with her toward them. He'd introduced her like they were lifelong friends of his.

The first one's name was Thunder. Solid black and bigger than any horse she'd ever seen, but oh, so gentle. She remembered how Thunder—who'd been eating at the time—had made his way over to Barry when they'd entered the pasture. When Barry rubbed his chin, he'd nodded and moved closer to him.

Barry had then pointed to two other horses nearby. Charger and Lucy. Their coloring reminded Priscilla of the nuts her mother placed on the dining room table every Christmas. And then there was a shorter gray one on the far side of the pasture. Her fear disappeared when she saw how gentle they were.

Until now, he'd been content with those four. Now he had seven.

She looked at Barry. "Why do I have the feeling that you didn't just stop at purchasing the horses?"

His brows rose. "I don't know what you mean."

"Will Jim wake up tomorrow and find a check in the mail? Anonymous? Perhaps for the exact amount his ranch needs to avoid bankruptcy?"

Barry looked at her but said nothing.

She walked over to him and wrapped her arms around his waist. "You're the most selfless person on earth, Barry King."

He smiled. "You give me too much credit. I know how it feels when your kids let you down. And I know what it's like to be on the cusp of losing everything." He shook his head. "What I did was selfish. I didn't want to see my friend travel down the same roads I had to."

"You're one of the best humans ever."

He looked down at her. "You're just saying that because I bought you a handsome new horse."

"I hope you purchased an instructor as well. Did you forget I don't know how to ride?"

"The instructor will be here Saturday morning at eight. Her name's Wilma."

Priscilla stepped back. "That's three days from now. You mean I can't ride Rich Brown until then? Can't you teach me?"

"No. I've picked up too many bad riding habits over the years. You're new to this and need to be trained properly. Whatever I teach you now, she'll just unteach you when she gets here. You can do everything else except ride him. Okay?"

"Everything else, like what?"

"Talk to him. Brush him."

"Walk him?"

"Only when one of the stable hands is around."

She folded her arms.

"I'll have one of them meet you out here tomorrow

morning. Rich Brown is gentle and used to being ridden, but he's only five years old. He still has a bit of fire in him. You'll need to earn his respect. Once you have that, I'll feel more comfortable about you working with him alone."

She looked over at Rich Brown, who stood quietly watching the other horses. "I don't think he'll give me any problems."

"Probably not. But right now, I'd rather play it safe."

His phone rang. He pulled it out of his pocket, looked at the screen, and showed it to her. It was his son, Grantham.

Barry put the phone back in his pocket.

A week ago, Priscilla ran into Grantham and his family while she was shopping. He'd never liked her, but he'd never publicly humiliated her, either. This time he'd walked up to her and made vile comments—loud enough for everyone to hear—about her past, how she used to make her living, and how she'd tricked his dad into marrying her. The last one was a lie, and she told him so. He then yanked the watch she was purchasing for Barry out of her hand, tossed it on the floor, and smashed it with his foot. Then he'd told the clerk that Priscilla didn't have the right to spend his dad's money.

Priscilla was so angry that when she arrived home, she didn't even know she'd been crying. When Barry saw her, he demanded to know what had happened. When she told him, he went to Grantham's home. At the time, she didn't know what happened or what was said, but found out later that Barry had fired Grantham from his company, King Global.

Grantham had been calling his dad's cell phone ever since and leaving messages—mainly begging his dad to answer. At first, the calls were just once a day. Now they were every hour.

Priscilla pulled Barry to her and laid her head on his chest. "Eventually, you're going to have to talk with him."

His body tensed. "I have nothing to talk to him about, Silly."

"He's offered to apologize to me."

"We both know it wouldn't be genuine. He's just doing everything he can to get his job back."

"I know. But I'm willing to let bygones be by—"

"No." He took a step back. "If you're willing to forgive him, that's fine. But don't sugarcoat what he did. I know you want us to make amends, but what he did was wrong. No one should be treated like that. Ever."

Priscilla agreed. She thanked God again that her mother hadn't been with her that day. It was no secret that Mabel hated every aspect of Priscilla's previous lifestyle, but there was no way she would've stood there and let Grantham treat her daughter that way. Grantham would've been the one running out of the store, not Priscilla.

She grimaced. She wasn't the running away type. Anyone who knew her knew she was the one who'd run straight toward trouble, not away from it. But Grantham was her husband's son. And Barry was more important to her than her pride. She didn't want to say or do anything to Grantham that would jeopardize that.

Barry's phone rang again. He retrieved it, tapped a button, and placed it back in his pocket.

"What did you just do?"

"Blocked his number. He knows I'm not going to answer, and now they're increasing in frequency."

Priscilla bowed her head. Grantham had already tried to visit his father, but had been turned away by security. Barry had told them that Grantham was no longer welcome on the estate. Now he was blocking his calls.

She swatted away a fly. If only she'd gone somewhere else that day. Perhaps to her girlfriends to vent, or to the store for a pint of ice cream. Something. She never should've come straight home.

He lifted her chin. "You didn't cause this, Silly, Grantham did. The way he's treated you over the years has gotten worse, not better. I'm done with it."

Priscilla sighed. She didn't like it, but Barry was right. No matter how hard she'd tried to establish a relationship with Grantham and his family, his behavior toward her had only become more aggressive. If he'd humiliate her in public, with his wife and kids looking on, what else was he capable of?

Rich Brown walked back over to her and lowered his head. He nudged her right hand with his muzzle. She scratched under his chin, its velvety softness contrasting with bristly whiskers. A minute later, he looked up at her and Priscilla wondered if the horse had somehow known what she'd been thinking.

"Well, look at that." Barry let out a chuckle. "I knew the two of you were made for each other. Welcome to the family, Rich Brown."

The horse tapped his right hoof on the ground again and whinnied. Priscilla laughed and kissed the horse on the nose before looking him in the eyes again.

She saw happiness and something else. Maybe it was a glimpse of that fire Barry had referred to earlier.

Her phone rang. She reached into her jean pocket and pulled it out. She squelched a fire of her own as she stared at the device while it continued to vibrate in her hand. The name taunted her from the screen.

Grantham.

Chapter 2

Priscilla handed the phone to Barry.

His eyes tightened. "Unbelievable."

In the three years she'd been married to his father, Grantham had never called her phone. She didn't even know he'd had the number.

But what upset her the most was that she knew what he was trying to do. He was going to play nice in order to get her to help smooth things over with his dad. But she wasn't having it. She wanted peace between them, but her days of being used were over.

Barry gripped the phone. "I'm putting a stop to this right now."

Priscilla grabbed his hand before he pressed the talk button. "No. Let it go unanswered. When he realizes we're on the same page, he'll stop."

Barry swiped her phone to the left and tapped a button before handing it back to her. "I blocked him from calling you as well." He clenched his jaw and stared out into the distance.

"What's wrong?"

"He's not going to stop until he gets his job back."

"Are you going to give it back to him?"

"No. But I am going to go see him. I'll stop by his place tomorrow morning on my way to the office."

Priscilla nodded. "Maybe that'll calm him down a little."

"It won't. The mansion that he and his family live in belongs to me. Tomorrow, I'm going to let him know that they have three days to find another place to live."

"You're throwing them out?"

He nodded, his gaze fixed on whatever he was looking at in the distance.

Priscilla gasped. "Barry, the children."

"Bobby and Shelly left yesterday. They're at that ridiculous prep school in Switzerland their mother always sends them to. They're fine."

Priscilla blew out a breath. "Barry, both of your children hate me. I can deal with Victoria's refusal to acknowledge our marriage, and I can deal with Grantham's obnoxious behavior. But if you do this, they'll hate me forever. There'll be no mending of relationships after that."

He shifted his gaze to her. "I told Grantham there'd be consequences if he continued to harass you."

"But Barry, they're going to—"

"I get it." He wrapped his hands around her forearms. "You think they're going to say that you put me up to this, but they won't. Edith and I taught them from an early age that for every action, there's a reaction. Victoria will be upset that I'm evicting her big brother, but she'll stay out of it. Grantham's worked for me for over twenty years and he's been paid very well. His family's not going to end up on the streets."

"If Edith was still alive, she'd never—"

"If she was still alive, I wouldn't have to."

"Still—"

"You're not gonna change my mind. I won't have

someone living in one of my properties and on my payroll who treats my wife like dirt."

"If only there was some way—"

"For us to be one big, happy family?"

"Listen, I'm not a fan of Grantham either at this point, but there's gotta be another way to make this work."

"For my sake?"

She nodded.

"Placating him isn't going to change how he feels about us being married." He shook his head. "Grantham's dislike of you stems from fear. And at the root of that stem is his love of money."

It was. She'd only had a few actual sit down conversations with Grantham over the years, and they were all centered on money. In his mind, Priscilla would get everything if something happened to his dad, and he'd be left with nothing.

Shields Canaan, one of the stable hands, walked toward them and reached for Rich Brown's lead rope. She and Barry watched quietly as Shields led Rich to the barn.

When the barn doors closed, Barry rubbed his chin. "What are your plans for tonight?"

"Tonight? I thought we were talking about your visit with Grantham tomorrow morning."

"The conversation was upsetting both of us, so how about we table it until later?"

His voice was light, but the muscles around his eyes and jaw were still tight. She'd been moments away from raising her voice and stomping off, so pressing pause was a good idea.

"Tonight, Liz and Lola will be stopping by. We're watching a movie."

He lowered his head and chuckled. "I've never seen you ladies watch any of the movies you pick out." He lifted his right hand and used it to mimic a mouth opening and closing. "All you do is talk, talk, talk."

"That's your fault." She curled her index finger around one of his belt loops and pulled him closer. "Since I've been married to you, I haven't spent as much time with them as I used to. I have to catch up with what's going on in their lives."

"You're not the only one who's married. So is Lola." His eyes widened. "I'll ask Ram to come with her. Then I'll ask his advice on the best way to handle Grantham tomorrow."

Ram was Lola's husband. Priscilla first met him several years ago when he'd started dating Lola. It wasn't until a couple of years later, when Priscilla met Barry, that she'd found out that Ram and Barry were good friends.

Grantham respected Ram and often referred to him as Uncle Ram. Priscilla wondered if it'd be a good idea for Ram to join Barry tomorrow.

Priscilla stomped her left foot to loosen a clump of dirt that had attached to the toe of her cowgirl boot. "I think Ram should actually go with you."

"Why?"

"Because I'm afraid of Grantham's reaction when you kick him out. He's hot-tempered and undoubtedly will say things to hurt you." Things like dragging her name through the mud. "You'll get angry and I don't even want to think about what could happen after that. Ram being there will make sure that cooler heads prevail."

Barry straightened his hat. "I'd rather you go with me."

She jerked back. "That would be a terrible idea." Not only would it fuel Grantham's suspicions that throwing his family out of the house was her idea, she also wasn't sure how many more of his accusations she'd be able to take without responding. "But if you want me to, I will."

He opened his hand, and she placed hers inside of it. He then waved at Shields and a few of the other stable hands before he led them out of the arena.

As they climbed the steps to the back porch, he said,

"I'd love to have you there. I don't want him to have any doubt about why he's being evicted." He opened the door that led into the kitchen. "But the more I think about it, the more I know you're right about it being a bad idea. Ram wouldn't mind tagging along."

She turned and looked up at him. No lights were on in the kitchen and the sun had set. She traced the line of his jaw with her finger. "Mama wanted me to help out at the café tomorrow, but I think I'm going to ask Lola to help instead. I'd like to be here when you get back."

"I'd like for you to be here, too. Will Mabel be okay with that?

"Absolutely. Lola, working as a waitress, is good for business."

He laughed. "Speaking of Lola, I'd better call Ram."

"The two of you are more than welcome to join us for movie night."

"I think we'll take a rain check on that. We'll probably go out for wings or something." He ran his fingers through her hair. "Do me a favor?"

"Anything."

"Call the house staff and tell them they have the day off tomorrow."

"Okay, but why?"

His eyes glinted.

"Oh, I see. You want me all to yourself tomorrow, is that it?"

He nodded and lowered his mouth toward hers.

The doorbell rang.

Priscilla stiffened. "That's Liz. She said she'd be stopping by early."

He leaned his forehead against hers and groaned. "Saved by the bell."

"Was I saved?" She kissed him until he pulled her tighter and moaned. "Or were you?"

Chapter 3

Priscilla handed Diamond Liz a glass bowl full of jellybeans.

Liz picked out a handful of the red ones. "Your face is flushed. What were you and Barry up to before I arrived?"

"Stop being nosey."

Liz giggled. "That tells me everything I need to know." She popped one of the red beans into her mouth, chewed, then tilted her head to the side. "Shall I leave and come back in an hour or so?"

Priscilla laughed and grabbed one of the throw pillows next to her on the couch. She aimed and tossed it toward Liz's shoulder. It bounced off the coffee table between them and landed at Liz's feet. "Wow. How is it possible that my aim is the same as it was when I was three?"

"You've never been able to throw, so I don't know why you tried." Liz pulled a purple jellybean out of the bowl and gave it an underhand toss. It landed in the center of Priscilla's lap. "*That's* how you do it."

Priscilla chewed the candy and reached for the bowl. Liz pulled out the remaining red ones before handing it to her.

Priscilla started to protest but smiled instead. She'd met Diamond Liz over a decade ago at a small, but very wild party. She'd intervened when Diamond Liz smacked the hand of another guest who'd tried to take one of her sugary red candies. That angry guest was now their best friend, Lola.

At the time, the three women had been hired by wealthy gentlemen to be their arm candy at certain events. And in some cases, paid a lot more for post-event activities. Priscilla plucked a white jellybean from the bowl and rolled it around with her fingers. It reminded her of the Scripture in the book of Isaiah that talked about sins being as scarlet, suddenly being white as snow. A feeling of love and forgiveness washed over her every time that Scripture came to mind. She blinked away tears. Her days of being "candy" for hire were long over, and so was Lola's.

Priscilla glanced at Liz. She wore white sneakers, a pair of light blue ripped jeans, and a soft pink T-shirt. Her long blonde hair laid over her shoulder and was secured by a gold hair clip with three diamonds in the center. Around her neck was a diamond solitaire necklace, and she wore a bracelet and ring that matched. Her friend Liz loved diamonds, hence her nickname. And she loved the lifestyle that supplied her with them.

Liz waved the diamond-studded arm in front of her. "Earth to Pris. Where'd you'd just go?"

"Down memory lane. Remembering how the three of us first met."

Liz smiled. "That was quite the night."

Priscilla sighed. "It was."

"Please don't start."

"Start what?"

"The lecture."

"I don't lecture you, Liz."

"You do. And the lectures have increased this past year,

so stop it because you do it all the time."

"*All* the time?"

"Yes."

Priscilla worried about her friend. She desperately wanted Liz to leave her lascivious lifestyle behind her, and she'd talked with her about it often. However, she wouldn't have called them lectures, but maybe that's how Liz was perceiving them.

"I worry about you."

Liz leaned back against the couch. "You and Lola found Jesus and walked away from that life and I'm happy the two of you have found … what did you call it? Peace?" She shrugged. "I don't need peace. I don't have any qualms about the way I've chosen to live my life."

"You've talked about walking away from it before."

"And I will. When I have a good reason to."

"But if—"

Liz raised her hand. "Please, Pris. Not tonight. I've had a hard week, and I've been looking forward to relaxing with you and Lola. Can we not start the evening off with an argument?"

Priscilla stared at her friend. Liz's eyes were the same brilliant blue they'd always been, but there was a sadness to them. She wasn't going to ask why. Liz wasn't the type to get up and leave if someone continued to pepper her with questions, but she would shut down. She hated when Liz did that. Not because it made her angry, but because it broke her heart. The deeper Liz withdrew into herself, the more lost she looked.

Priscilla stood. "You're right. It's been almost a month since I've seen you." She walked around the coffee table and plopped on the sofa next to Liz. She was about to hug her when her phone dinged. She pulled it out of her pocket. "Lola and Ram just pulled up."

"Ram? I didn't know he was coming."

"He's not. Well, not really. He's here for Barry."

Liz nodded and picked out another handful of jellybeans. The black ones this time.

Priscilla picked up the pillow that had landed at Liz's feet, then they tidied up the rest of the parlor before heading to the kitchen. Priscilla pulled a bag of pretzels from the cabinet, then three bottles of ginger ale from the refrigerator. The movie room had a popcorn maker and the rest of the snacks they'd need.

"Hello, ladies." Ram burst through the kitchen entrance, which was the one their close friends and family used. Lola bounded in behind him. He nodded to Priscilla. "Wanted to say hi before I disappeared with your husband." He waved at Liz. She returned the wave, asking, "Where are you guys headed?"

"Gonna grab a few burgers and wings, then head over to the Habakkuk Sports Complex. A couple of local teams are having a baseball tournament there."

Liz smiled. "That sounds like fun. Pris, what do you think about crashing in on their little adventure?"

Liz was teasing, and Priscilla played along. "I think it'd be fun. Don't you, Lola?"

"Leave my man alone." Lola wrapped golden-brown arms around Ram's waist. "Ignore them, baby. Go have fun. And don't forget to bring me back one of those cute little hats."

He chuckled. "You mean cap." He gave her a kiss on the nose. "And I won't forget."

Priscilla looked at Liz, who pretended to gag.

Ram said his goodbyes, and Lola closed the door behind him. She turned toward Priscilla and Liz and placed a hand on her perfectly curved hip. "Are you crazy? Why were you ladies trying to get us stuck at a baseball game?"

Priscilla shook her head. "He knew we were teasing. No way would they have agreed to let us tag along."

Lola giggled, and short, shiny brown ringlet curls danced when she did. "My husband plays the long game."

She pinched two fingers together. "He was *this* close to phoning Barry and calling your bluff." She waved a hand over her dress. "And do I look like I'm dressed to go watch men play in the dirt?"

She wore a sleeveless, multi-layered, sky blue maxi dress. The top layer was covered by a thin layer of chiffon. And she was barefoot. She was always barefoot.

Lola dressed a lot more conservatively now than she had in the past, but no matter how hard she tried, she still wasn't able to mask the natural hourglass curves underneath. Priscilla sighed. Life so wasn't fair.

A knock at the kitchen door pulled her from her thoughts and she motioned for Lola to open it. "That's probably Barry letting us know they're leaving."

Lola opened the door, but it wasn't Barry standing there. It was Shields, their stable hand.

When he saw Lola, he took a step back. "I'm sorry. I was looking for Mr. King."

Priscilla stepped to the door. "Hi, Shields."

"Oh. Hi, Mrs. King. Sorry to bother you. I saw the light on and thought—"

"It's okay. Barry's left for the evening and I'm just spending some time with friends." She pointed to her left. "This is Lola."

Shields had a pair of baseball cleats in one hand and a jersey in the other. He laid the jersey across his arm and extended his hand to Lola. He greeted her, but his gaze was focused behind them.

Priscilla turned and was startled to see Liz standing right behind them, her eyes locked on Shields. Was she blushing?

She pushed Liz in front of her. "And this is Elizabeth Decker."

"Please call me Liz."

He smiled and reached for her hand. "Nice to meet you, Liz. I'm Shields. Shields Canaan."

They continued to stare at each other.

Priscilla cleared her throat.

"I'm sorry." Shields glanced at his watch. "I should go. Hope I didn't interrupt your evening too much, ladies." He nodded at Lola, then Liz. "It was nice meeting both of you."

Liz pointed to his cleats. "You play baseball?"

"I do. For the Habakkuk Lions." He glanced at his watch again. "I really should get going. We have a game in a couple of hours."

Liz nodded.

He walked toward the steps, stopped, then turned to face the door again. "I have a couple of free tickets if you ladies would be interested in going."

Lola looked at her feet. "I'm not dressed for a game, and there's no way Pris will sit on a pair of bleachers on a hot August night like this. But Liz would love to go."

A smile spread across Shields' face. "Liz, would you like to go to the game with me?"

Pink tinged her cheeks. "I would."

Priscilla whispered in her ear. "I thought you were looking forward to spending girl time with us?"

Liz waved her away.

Shields clasped Liz's hand, and they jogged down the steps.

Priscilla stepped onto the porch and watched as they walked toward his truck, which he'd apparently left in front of the barn.

Lola pulled Priscilla inside and closed the door. Her dark brown eyes now danced along with her curls. "This is so exciting! Pris, I think we just witnessed one of our prayers being answered."

"What?"

"Didn't you tell me Shields is a Christian?"

"No. I said he's been asking Barry a lot of questions about the Christian faith."

Lola rubbed her hands together. "That's good. He

wouldn't be asking about Christianity if he didn't believe there's a God."

"That's a very glass-is-half-full way of thinking about it."

Lola nodded and pointed to her heart. "I feel it. Diamond Liz meeting Shields Canaan is going to be life-changing for her. In a good way. We've prayed for this, Pris. We both knew something huge would have to happen in order for Liz to change her life, and Mr. Tall-with-dark-waves is that change. Did you see the way he looked at her? The way she looked at him? The electricity between them was palpable. Not only that, everyone knows I'm a good judge of character and *I* say that Shields is a good man. Who knew that *I* would be the one to help Liz find love?"

Priscilla grabbed two of the bottles of ginger ale and handed one to Lola. "You didn't. He stopped by *my* house, remember?"

"Who's gonna remember that little detail?" She popped the top off of her ginger ale and took a sip. "All Shields and Diamond will remember is that I was the one who introduced them."

Priscilla laughed. "That's not what happened."

Lola winked at her. "In my retelling of the story, it will be."

They made their way down the stairs that led to the theater room. Priscilla continued to tease Lola about the flaws in her story but she wasn't able to join Lola in her excitement. She wanted to, but she couldn't. Not fully.

Priscilla hoped Shields would be the "good reason" Liz needed to leave the past behind her.

But Shields had a past as well. And it wasn't a good one.

Chapter 4

Priscilla looked at the digital display on her treadmill. Three more miles.

She thought about hitting the plus sign to add another two, but her thighs had been bothering her ever since her impromptu horse ride earlier that morning.

Her alarm went off as usual at 5:00 a.m. but when she reached for Barry, he hadn't been there. He'd left a note saying that he was meeting Ram for prayer and an early morning breakfast before heading to Grantham's.

She'd tried to pray herself after that but kept being distracted by the what-if's. What if Ram going along wasn't a good idea after all? Maybe what Grantham and Barry needed was time alone. Space to air their grievances. It was no secret that Grantham had a lot he wanted to say to his father. Would Ram being there hinder that? What if time alone was what Barry and Grantham needed to heal?

What if Ram wasn't able to stop their anger from boiling over? What if he got hurt? Would Lola ever forgive her? Would Barry?

After an hour of wrestling with her thoughts, she rolled

out of bed and slid on a pair of jeans and a long-sleeve tee. She then walked into her shoe closet and lifted the lid on a box she'd stumbled over last night when she was getting ready for bed. Inside the box was a brand-new pair of women's riding boots, with a note attached. The gift was from Barry. He must've placed them in her closet while she was visiting with Liz and Lola.

She'd pulled on the sleek-black boots and made her way to the arena. She'd then asked Francine—one of the female stable hands—to get Rich Brown ready to ride. When the woman hesitated, Priscilla had assured her she wasn't going to ride Rich Brown. She just wanted to get used to sitting in a saddle.

Francine agreed. She had also agreed to let Priscilla sit behind her while Francine rode Rich Brown around the arena a few times. Priscilla learned Francine had the heart of a teacher. Everything she'd done, she'd explained to Priscilla why she was doing it. Francine had talked incessantly, and Priscilla had tried her best to soak it all in. It had been a great distraction from her thoughts about Barry and what was happening at Grantham's home.

Priscilla looked down at the display again. Only half-a-mile to go. She ran faster and huffed out a few breaths before glancing at her watch. It was almost noon, and Barry still wasn't home. She lifted a corner of the towel that was around her neck, blotted her forehead, and jumped when she felt a hand on her waist.

She reached for the handrail to steady her balance, but it was too late. She braced for the impact of her face hitting the iron bar at the bottom of the display board.

The hand on her waist slid off and was replaced by two hands that lifted her off of the treadmill.

When her feet touched the floor, she spun around. "Barry! Oh, my word. You startled me."

"I know. I'm sorry." He punched several buttons on the display board, and the treadmill slowed to a halt. "You didn't have your earbuds in, so I thought you heard me approaching. Are you okay?"

She placed her hands on her knees. "Need a second to catch my breath."

He pulled the towel from her neck and dried the sweat that rolled down her arms. "You had that thing at top speed. I asked you to stop doing that. One misstep at that speed can land you in the E.R."

Priscilla blew out a breath. "And it probably would have if you hadn't intervened. After you warned me about it, I set it to a lower speed. I only turned it up today so I could focus on running and not on you and Grantham."

She inhaled a breath, blew it out, then straightened to look at Barry. He had a cut on his bottom lip. Her heart rate increased again. "What happened? Did Grantham hit you?"

He touched the cut. "It looks worse than it is."

"You didn't answer my question."

"No, he did not hit me."

"Then what happened?"

"Ram stayed in the car, and I went in to talk with Grantham. I told him why I was there, and that he had three days to pack up his family's stuff and leave." Barry's jaw tightened. "He then started yelling and calling you every name in the book. Because of that, I told him they had to be out by midnight tonight instead." He rubbed his forehead. "That's when Ram came in and asked if we were all right. Grantham grabbed a nine iron and started smashing the windows. I pulled out my phone to call the Sheriff, then Grantham tried to wrestle the phone away from me."

"So he didn't intentionally hit you?"

"He didn't hit me at all. Ram accidentally did when he stepped between us."

"Is he okay?"

"He will be."

"Barry."

"Silly, everyone's alive and breathing, all right?"

Priscilla normally smiled when he used the nickname Silly, because it always brought back memories of their first days together. Her friends and family had shortened her name to Pris a long time ago, but Barry was never a fan of that one and chose Silly instead, saying it was also a shortened version of her name.

The tone that usually accompanied the nickname Silly was soft and sensual. Now it was tired.

"And it's over." Barry leaned back against the treadmill. "I have movers over at the house moving Grantham's and his family's things out right now, and my lawyer will deal with the other situation."

"What situation?"

"Grantham was arrested for property damage."

"What?"

"He was arr—"

"Wait. Who called the police?"

"I did."

"I thought he wrestled the phone away from you?"

"I said he *tried* to wrestle it from me. He wasn't successful."

Priscilla wasn't surprised, and she wondered why Grantham had even tried. She was only fifty-three, but Barry had already passed his seventieth year—though no one could tell that by looking at him. He was a former bodybuilder and kept in shape by lifting weights and working out daily. Grantham, on the other hand, reminded her of the Pillsbury Doughboy.

"The Sheriff asked if I wanted to press charges. I said yes."

"Barry, please don't. That'll make the whole situation worse. I'm sure when he calms down he'll—"

"Silly," the softened tone was back again. "The past couple of hours have been rough. Can we pick up this conversation later?"

She looked up at him. There was a lot more she wanted

to say, but his disheveled hair, dim eyes, and sullen cheeks told her this wasn't the right time. Right now, he didn't need her words, opinions, and thoughts. He needed *her*. He needed the love and tender care that only she could provide.

She wrapped her arms around him and laid her head against her favorite place in the world—his chest. "We can pick up that conversation later or never. I trust you, Barry. Grantham is your son and despite the way he's been acting, I know you love him and would do nothing to hurt him. The measures you're taking seem drastic to me, but I've only known him for a couple of years—you've known him his entire life. Every day, you show me I'm just as important, so whatever decision you make, I'll support it because I know you only want the best for him. And for me."

His muscles visibly relaxed before he kissed the top of her head and lifted her chin. "It means a lot to me to hear you say that."

He kissed her gently on the lips and wrapped his arms around her.

Priscilla had found out in her twenties that she'd never be able to bear children. She had no idea what it took to parent an adult child, but Barry did, and judging by the look in his eyes, it was hard.

Real hard.

He'd never asked Victoria or Grantham to like her, only to respect her. Their refusal to honor that simple request broke his heart. They both had been close to their mother, who'd passed away a few years before Priscilla met Barry. He was a widower when they met, but because of her past and his wealth, rumors had poisoned Grantham's and Victoria's minds long before they'd ever met her.

Barry knew her past would be a stumbling block for them, so together they'd given them the space they needed, and prayed and hoped that one day they'd all be able to talk it over and function together as a family.

However, instead of talking it over, Victoria and

Grantham started investigations. Several of them. Not only into Priscilla, but into Mama and Penelope as well. Of course, they couldn't find anything on either of them, and it was Barry who'd initially told them about Priscilla's past, but it didn't matter. They continued to dig deeper and sunk to depths she'd never thought they'd sink to—like contacting a former client of Priscilla's and having him call their dad.

Barry handled the entire incident with a lot more grace than she would've if the shoe had been on the other foot. He also said nothing to Grantham or Victoria about it afterward.

But Grantham harassing her in public had been the last straw. She'd never seen Barry so angry at one of his children before, and the result of that had led to this moment.

A husband and father in her arms, battling a battle he shouldn't have to fight.

Who would win? Would it be her? Or his children?

Either way, it wouldn't be a win for Barry.

She inhaled his woodsy scent and pulled him closer. It was all her fault. She should've walked away when she realized Victoria and Grantham would never accept her. Barry had done everything in his power to not let the relationship with his children affect their marriage. He'd sacrificed so much.

She feared the day would come when she'd have to make a sacrifice, too. She wiped away a tear because she didn't know if she'd be able to do it.

No. She would do it.

She'd do anything for the man she loved.

Chapter 5

Priscilla carefully sat on the bed next to Barry.

She wanted to kiss his lips, but his back was to her. Instead, she ran her fingers through his salt-and-pepper hair. It had always reminded her of silk. Today, it reminded her he desperately needed a haircut.

He moaned but didn't open his eyes.

She lowered the sheets and gently raked her nails across his back. For the three years they'd been married, she couldn't recall one time that he'd actually slept with a shirt on. She didn't mind. It allowed her to look at his ripped muscles and six-pack all night long.

He moaned again, then turned toward her and smiled. Then he frowned.

"Where are you going this early?"

She pointed to the riding boots she was wearing.

He sat up on his elbow. "Today's Saturday?"

"No. It's Thursday." She giggled. "Did you really think that we'd slept for two days straight?"

Red spread across his cheeks. "Well—"

"Nevermind." Yesterday, after his visit to Grantham's,

they'd retired to the bedroom early. Really early. It had only been one o'clock.

He narrowed his eyes. "Why are you wearing your boots if it's Thursday? The riding instructor said the earliest she could be here was Saturday."

She chewed at her lip before answering. "I kind of went riding yesterday."

"Tell me you're kidding."

She held up a hand. "But I wasn't alone. I asked one of the stable hands to let me ride with them. I never touched the reins."

"Who'd you ask?"

"Francine."

He nodded, and his demeanor softened. "Francine's finaled in several dressage competitions. She's good and knows a lot about horses. If I'd had the chance to choose a hand to ride with you, it would've been her." His brow wrinkled. "But I didn't know you were planning to do that, Silly. I wish you would've told me. Horses are dangerous, honey. If I'd come home and found you'd gotten hurt—"

"Francine took excellent care of me. And I wasn't planning on doing that. I just wanted to practice getting in the saddle, but one thing led to another and I just wanted to see what it'd be like to ride him. I wanted to call and let you know, but I didn't want to interrupt you and Grantham."

"Francine should've called."

"I told her I'd be the one to talk to you."

He rubbed the back of his neck.

"Don't be mad at her. I'm the one who talked her into it." She placed Barry's hand in hers and kissed it. "Forgive me?"

He blew out a breath and chuckled. "Silly, what am I going to do with you?"

"Let me go riding again today?"

He shook his head. "Francine doesn't work on Thursdays."

"Phooey." Barry had three more women who worked with the horses, but she'd liked the connection she'd made with Francine. She also liked the way Francine taught while talking about other things at the same time.

"I'm sorry, honey. I can ride with you later this evening if you'd like."

"That'll be great, thanks." She scooted closer to him on the bed. "There's something else I need to tell you."

"Careful. You want Francine to keep her job, right?"

"It's nothing like that. It's about one of your male stable hands."

He tossed his pillow aside and sat up. "Which one?"

"Shields."

His eyes narrowed. "Did he say something to you or—"

"No. I mean, yes. He came by looking for you the night Liz and Lola were here."

"Yeah, he told me. Ram and I stopped by the Lions' locker room after the game and congratulated them on their win. He said he'd wanted to let me know about one of the fences needing to be repaired."

"Well, when he was here, he really hit it off with Liz. He even invited her to go to the game."

"Yeah?"

Priscilla nodded. "Did you see her there?"

"No. Ram and I hung out with the team for an hour and then headed back here." He scratched his chin. "But now that I think about it, Shields didn't stay. He'd grabbed a shower and left immediately after."

"Does Shields work today?"

"This afternoon he does. Why?"

"I was wondering if you could talk to him about Liz."

The look on Barry's face told her he was waiting to hear more. She cleared her throat. "I've talked to Liz. It's only been a few days, but she's been spending a lot of time with Shields. She likes him a lot. And from what she's been telling me, he feels the same way. But … have you ever told Shields about my past?"

"No. Why would I?"

Of course, Barry had never said anything to Shields. She gave herself a mental slap for asking such a stupid question. He'd never do that without talking to her first. "It's just that … I wonder how he's going to react when he finds out what Liz does for a living."

Barry ran a hand through his hair, then shook his head. "I think it's too early for you to worry about that. They've known each other for less than a week."

"She's smitten, Barry. I've never seen her like this before. She's already talking about what their future might look like."

"Their future doesn't look good. I pay all the stable hands well, but not well enough to support the lifestyle Liz is used to. Especially Shields."

"What do you mean?"

"The first thing Shields asked after I hired him was for me to send eighty percent of his pay directly to the Collins Family."

Collins. As in Ashley Collins, the fourteen-year-old girl who was paralyzed from the waist down because of a drunken driver. Shields Canaan had been that driver.

Barry continued, "He's lived off of twenty percent of his pay for the past five years. He has a small one-bedroom home and a truck, but those are his only assets. Although, he's joked several times about claiming his Doberman, Rocco, as a dependent on his taxes."

"Was the eighty percent a judgment from the court?"

"No. The state was satisfied after he'd done his time in prison. That's something he does on his own to help the Collins family with Ashley's medical expenses."

Wow. She'd had no idea.

"The family didn't ask for it, either. They've told both me and Shields that a fund has been set up by their church to take care of whatever balance is left on Ashley's medical bills after their insurance pays, but he sends the money anyway."

Barry climbed out of the bed. Priscilla smiled at the dancing hearts on his pajama pants and handed him his bathrobe from a nearby chair. He slid it on and continued, "Shields is a good guy. He's made plenty of mistakes, but he's taken responsibility for all of them. However, that doesn't leave a lot left over for Liz."

He was right. Right now, Liz was head-over-heels with her new guy, but how long would that last? Shields wasn't poor, but according to Barry, he was close to it. Shields had made the choice to live on a small amount of his earnings so that he'd be able to ease the burdens of the Collins family. That warmed her heart. It told her that money wasn't important to him. Doing the right thing was.

Would he choose to do the right thing with Liz?

If he did, what would that look like?

What would be the right thing to do?

Chapter 6

It was Friday and Priscilla couldn't be happier.

She tied the laces on her running shoes, then grabbed a small backpack and her keys from the nook in the foyer. She was meeting Liz for an early morning jog in the park, then she was meeting her friends Windy and Christianna later to get a jump on Christmas shopping.

The fall season hadn't officially started yet, but it was close. Priscilla pressed the remote to unlock her car door and hurried inside. It wouldn't be long before she'd have to use the remote starter. Maybe this year, she'd actually start parking her Volvo in the garage. Barry had never understood why she'd preferred parking in the driveway, and she'd never understood why he preferred to park in the garage. But if the Farmer's Almanac was correct, the upcoming winter was going to be a bad one. She may actually *have* to park inside for once.

She adjusted the heat and pulled onto the main road that led to the highway. A quick glance at the sky showed that the sun was just about to peek over the horizon. Good. The park rangers were strict about not letting anyone into the park until after sunrise. This way, she and Liz wouldn't have to wait. They'd be able to start as soon as they got there.

Her eyes flicked to her rearview mirror. A black sedan with New York plates came up fast behind her. She looked at her speedometer. The speed limit was thirty-five, and she was doing thirty. Whoever was behind her was obviously not familiar with this road. If they were, they wouldn't be in such a hurry. Logton—the main road from her house to the highway—had sharp turns and steep hills. It had two-lanes, but because of the many blind spots, a long stretch of the road had been designated a no-passing zone. She kept her speed steady. She wasn't going to end up in a ditch because of someone else's impatience.

She tightened her seat belt and looked in the rearview mirror again. The sedan was on her tail. What in the world?

The sedan sped up and rammed her car. She gripped the steering wheel. What in the blazes were they doing? They must be crazy!

She looked over her shoulder to get a look at the driver, but the windows to the sedan were tinted. She couldn't tell if there was one person inside or two. She swallowed. There could even be more.

She turned her attention back to the road. Two miles ahead, the road would widen a bit and she'd be able to pull to the side and let the idiots behind her pass. Until then, she needed to increase the distance between her car and theirs as much as possible. She pressed the accelerator. A dangerous turn was coming up, but every fiber of her being told her she needed to get far away from the crazy people behind her.

She slowed as she approached the curve, but the sedan sped up and rammed into the back of her car again. She gripped the wheel and tried to turn into the curve, but ended up angled sideways. The sedan pushed her car to the edge of the road. She screamed as the car teetered above a steep incline.

The engine of the sedan revved up, and she screamed

again as her car tumbled down the incline and towards the creek below it. *"Lord, please don't let my life end like this."* She closed her eyes and continued to pray as the car rolled. When it stopped, she opened her eyes. The air bag had deployed and it had blood on it. Something dripped into her eyes. She wiped across her forehead and looked at her hand. More blood.

She dabbed at her eyes with her sleeve, then grabbed the door handle and opened it. Water filled the car. She tried to close it again, but her arm had lost its strength.

She needed help.

Her phone. It was in her backpack. She'd call for help, then call Barry. Because if the pain in her head was an indicator, it may be the last time she'd get to speak to him.

Her feet were cold. Was it from the water flowing across them? Or something else?

She sucked in a deep breath and reached for the backpack she'd tossed into the passenger seat earlier. Her head pounded, but she had to get to the phone that was inside it. She pulled the pack closer but her fingers weren't able to unzip it. They were cold and numb. *"Lord,"* she whispered. *"I need Your help. I have to get to this phone. No one will see my car from the road. Nobody'll know I'm down here. I have to call for help."*

She tried the zipper again and cried when her fingers failed to hold on to the clasp.

The tears made her headache worse. Good. She needed to stop crying anyway and focus on getting out of the car before she drowned.

She sat up straighter and her vision dimmed. *"No, Lord. Please ... no. I need to be able to see so that I can find a way out of here."*

Her body shook. The water had reached her knees. It was like sitting in a tomb of ice.

"Help me, Jesus." The words shuddered out of her mouth, and her lids were heavy. The dimness turned dark

gray. She refused to shut her eyes. She had to stay awake. She had to fight. She had to …

The gray turned dark. Her lids closed slowly and she breathed out, *"Your will be done, Lord."*

"Your will be done."

Chapter 7

"**Time for you** to wake up, Prissy. Time for you to wake up."

Priscilla coughed and opened her eyes. "Mama?"

"Yes, daughter, it's me." Mabel grabbed her hand and gently squeezed it. "You were in a car accident this morning. Now you're in the hospital, but you're going to be okay."

"No, mama." Priscilla coughed again and shook her head. "It wasn't an accident. Someone ran me off the road."

Mabel nodded. "We know. There was another car on the road and that driver saw the whole thing. He's the one who called 911. He was even able to give the police a partial plate number and description of the car."

"Someone saw what happened?"

"Yes, a teenager on his way to work. It took him a minute to get down the rocky incline, but he had a 911 operator on the phone the whole time. He told them the car was filling with water and they instructed him on what to do until help arrived."

Priscilla chuckled.

Mabel frowned. "What's so funny?"

"I kept begging the Lord to help me. Little did I know, help was already on the way."

Her mom smiled. "We serve a mighty God."

"We do, Mama. We do." Priscilla looked around the room. "Barry. I need to call him. He doesn't know what happened. I don't want him to—"

"Shhh." Mabel patted her hand. "Don't get all riled up now. Barry's here, and he knows what happened. He's right down the hall talking with your doctors."

Priscilla swallowed. "Why? Am I going to be okay?"

"You have a nasty gash on your forehead, and you were unconscious for a while, but the doctors have assured us you're going to be fine. They're keeping you overnight for observation. Barry's just talking with them about the next steps after that."

Priscilla closed her eyes and thanked God that she wasn't able to make that sad and frantic call to Barry. He would've been worried sick. And with everything that's going on with his children right now, the last thing she wanted was to add additional stress. She opened her eyes. "How did the two of you find out what happened?"

"Liz. When you didn't show up at the park, she called your cell phone. The young man—Steven is his name—answered and told her what happened. After that, she called Barry and then me."

Priscilla fought back tears. God was merciful. She remembered praying throughout the whole ordeal, but she also remembered there was a part of her that thought her last breath would be taken in what was sure to be a cold and watery grave.

"Were the police able to find out who did it?"

Mabel's eyes tightened. "Yes, and no."

"What do you mean?"

"With the information Steven gave them, they found out that the car was a rental from out of state. But whoever rented it used a fake name and ID. They're still investigating."

Priscilla studied her mom's face. Something was wrong. "Mama, what aren't you telling me?"

"Yesterday morning, after my prayer time, I had a vision. I know who's responsible for your accident."

Mama'd had visions for as long as Priscilla could remember. They didn't happen often, perhaps every couple of years, but throughout the years Priscilla had learned to pay attention to them.

"What did you see, Mama?"

Mabel looked out the window. "I'd like to pray about it some more." She spun back to Priscilla. "Until then, I want you to stay away from …" Her mother shook her head. "Nevermind. I'll be staying by your side until this person is arrested. I'm not going to let them get anywhere near you again. Not on my watch."

Priscilla sucked in a breath and debated if she should demand more information from her mom or let it go. If she pushed hard enough, her mom may let a name slip, but then what? What could she do with the information? She wouldn't be able to tell the police because they'd want to know why she suspected that person. She couldn't tell them it was because her mom had a vision. Well, she could, but would that be more helpful or harmful to the investigation? No doubt, they'd ask Mom about it, and she'd say God showed it to her in a vision. Would they take her seriously? Probably not, but even if they did, what would they be able to do about it? More importantly, what would it do to the investigation? Would they think that she and her mom were looney and drop it?

No. She trusted her mom and her visions. Mama would tell her and the police when she was absolutely certain and not before. Her mother wasn't the type to be afraid of pointing the finger at someone, but she'd never point it unjustly. She'd wait on the Lord and speak then.

But her mother had made one thing clear. It was

unintentional, but clear nonetheless.

The person who'd tried to kill her was no stranger.

Chapter 8

Priscilla clenched Barry's hand as he lowered her into the plush, oyster-colored, swivel recliner. She'd initially balked at the bulky piece when they'd decided to redecorate their bedroom, but Barry and the salesperson had convinced her to give it a try. She was glad she did. It was like sitting on a cloud.

A year ago, when they'd purchased it, she'd had no idea how much of a blessing it'd be to her today. The bucket seat, sloping padded arms, and adjustable footrest were exactly what she needed right now. It had been seven days since the accident, and she'd spent the last five of those days medicated and asleep in her bed. Her muscles were still sore, but she was done lying down. She needed to sit up, and she needed a cup of coffee.

Barry pulled a fluffy peach throw from the bedroom closet and laid it across her. "It matches your gown."

Priscilla adjusted the throw around her. Her nightgown was made of cotton, had long sleeves, and gathered at her ankles, but it wasn't the warmest of sleepwear. She hadn't been outside since Barry and her mom brought her home from the hospital, but a quick glance outside the bedroom window let her know the temperature had dipped. And judging from the frost on some of the tree branches, it had dropped significantly.

Barry slid thick, Sherpa-lined socks onto her feet and stood. "I still think it's too early for you to move about. The doctors said bed rest is the best thing for you right now."

She leaned back in the recliner. "I am resting. I've been bedridden for days. I just need a change."

He sighed and walked over to the dresser. When he reached for the pain medicine the doctor had prescribed, she swiveled toward him. "I don't need those, babe. I'm okay."

"You're not okay." He shook two pills into his hand and placed the bottle back on the dresser. "I saw the look on your face when we walked from the bed to the chair."

Doggone, he'd seen it. She'd have to do a better job of masking it. Especially now, since the swivel action was making her head pound.

"They get rid of the pain, Barry, but they also knock me out for hours. I don't want to be in a pill-induced coma. I want to be aware of what's happening around me and feel alive. Those make me feel like life's passing me by."

He crouched in front of the chair. "What hurts?"

"What do you mean?"

"You're squinting. What hurts?"

Blast it. She *really* needed to work on her poker face. "My head. But it only started hurting when I turned the chair and the pain is already subsiding."

He lifted the pills to her lips, but she tightened them and turned her head like a three-year-old child. He tickled the bottom of her foot and when she laughed, he popped them into her mouth.

"That's not fair." She mumbled around the pills.

"All's fair in love and war. Now swallow."

She pointed to a glass of water on the nightstand. "I need water."

"They're coated. You'll be fine."

She pinched her lips together and swallowed, the bitter aftertaste making her suck her cheeks in. She opened her mouth wide to show Barry.

He patted her knee and walked toward the nightstand. "You'll feel better in no time."

"I *feel* like you're not hearing me."

"I hear you." He grabbed the glass of water and handed it to her. "No one wants you to feel more alive than I do, but I also know you're in pain." He gently lifted the bandage on her forehead. "Dr. Greengold has already talked about lowering the dosage. I'll give him a call after I change this bandage."

"Where's Mama?"

"Downstairs, praying up a storm with Lydia."

"Lydia's here? Barry, why didn't you tell me?"

"Because she didn't come here to see you. She arrived this morning before dawn and has been huddling and praying with Mabel ever since."

Priscilla glanced at the wall clock next to the window. It was eight a.m. "Lydia's been here for three hours, and she hasn't asked to see me?"

"She's seen you every day that you've been home. So have Liz, Lola, Windy, and the rest of your friends. So has Penelope."

She tilted her head to the side.

Barry stood in front of her again. "You were asleep when they came."

"My friends and sister were here and you didn't wake me?"

"I wanted to, but they all said they wanted you to rest."

Priscilla ignored the urge to yell. Barry should've woken her up, anyway. She would've loved the opportunity to chat with her friends and family. But right now, she didn't need the throbbing in her head to start up again.

He lifted her hand and kissed it. "Let me get started on

changing this bandage."

"I want Mama to do it."

He took a step back. "You don't like the way I do it?"

"She hums when she does it."

"You like my singing."

"She doesn't sing, she hums. You're a horrible hummer."

He chuckled. "I didn't know one could be bad at humming."

"Mama's humming is soft and relaxing. Your humming is chainsaw-like."

"Okay." He folded his arms across his chest. "Maybe my humming is bad, but that's not what this is about. You're mad at me."

She hiked a brow.

He kissed the top of her head. "Fine. I'll go get your mother."

Priscilla reached for his arm. "Only if they're done praying."

He blew out a breath. "It may be awhile, then. They're either whispering to each other, anointing the house with oil or …"

"Or what?"

He pressed one of the power buttons on the recliner and waited patiently until Priscilla was upright. She was glad he'd pushed the third one. The first two would've given her a migraine, for sure.

"Silly, did you know the guys in the car that hit you?"

She stopped her head from flinching back. "No. Well, I never saw their faces, so I don't really know for sure. Why are you asking?"

"Does Mabel know?"

Priscilla sucked in a breath. Mama did know. Or at least she believed she did. Priscilla wanted to answer Barry's question, but he'd want a name, and she didn't have one. Not yet. Was that what her Mom and Lydia were downstairs praying about?

"Barry, I—"

"Mabel's never shied away from praying around me. Most of the time she asks if I'd like to join her, and I have on many occasions. And Lydia and I pray together all the time with our group at church. But when I asked if I could join them this morning, they hesitated."

"Did they say why?"

"No, but I got the feeling that they're keeping something from me. And I think it has to do with your accident."

Priscilla rubbed the back of her neck. Was her mother trying to keep something from Barry? If so, what? Her mother wasn't one for secrets, and she definitely wouldn't hold back on telling Barry about her vision. Of course, he'd want a name, but he'd understand when she'd explain that she wanted to be sure. But to keep him out of the loop entirely? What was going on?

Priscilla looked into Barry's eyes. There was concern there, not doubt, and her heart melted. If he'd thought her past had come back to haunt them once again, he didn't show it. But the question remained. Was it someone from her past? She'd spent time with many a scum back in the day, but none of them wanted her dead.

And none of them had ever met her mother.

But whoever it was, her mother was definitely familiar with them.

Priscilla bit her lip. Was her mom hesitant to share with Barry because it involved him?

Did Barry know the men who'd tried to kill her?

Chapter 9

"Wake up, sleepyhead."

Priscilla yawned and forced her eyelids open. She'd remembered them feeling heavy when she'd talked with Barry. She must've fallen asleep. Again.

Liz sat on a stool in front of her. "I was content to sit here and watch you sleep, but Barry said you'd want me to wake you. I take it you haven't been a very good patient."

"I'm resting like the doctor said, but it's these blasted pain meds." She lowered the footrest and adjusted the recliner until she was sitting upright again. Apparently, Barry had put it in the sleep position when the prescription kicked in. She wondered if she'd actually fallen asleep while talking to him.

She stretched. "What time is it?"

"Two p.m."

She'd been knocked out for almost six hours. She wiped at her eyes. "Thanks for waking me."

"How do you feel?"

She slowly moved her head back and forth and rolled her shoulders. She then twisted her lower back a bit. Those were the spots that were giving her grief earlier. Nothing caused her to wince or cry out in pain. Hmph. Maybe those hours of sleep hadn't been a complete waste of time after all.

"I feel good, actually. How long have you been here?"

"Just a few minutes. Do you need to go to the bathroom or anything?"

"I do, but it can wait. I feel like I haven't seen you in forever. How are things going with you?"

"Now that you're okay? Great. But the day that guy answered your phone? Terrible. It was one of the scariest days of my life."

"I'm sorry you had to hear about what happened that way."

"Up until that point, I just thought you were running late." Liz clicked her tongue. "I wish I had known. Maybe there was something I could've done."

"You did do something. You called Barry and Mama. You knew how important making those calls would be for me."

"I also drove to the scene, but the police wouldn't let me through. That was frustrating because I didn't want you to think that you were alone."

"Thank you for showing up, though. It means a lot."

Liz lowered her eyes. "Do you have any idea who'd want to—"

"I don't." Priscilla blinked away the rest of the sleep from her eyes. "But let's not talk about the accident anymore." She tilted her head to the side and smiled. "I want to talk about you. How are things with you and Shields? I feel like I've missed out on a whole lifetime of news about the two of you."

Liz's cheeks turned red. "Shields is …" She shook her head and beautiful blond waves bounced and twisted on her shoulders. Odd. Liz normally wore her hair parted down the middle and straight. Now she had a side part and beach waves framed her face. Interesting.

"Shields is absolutely wonderful, Pris. I mean, I know it's only been a few weeks but … well, how does the name Elizabeth Canaan sound?"

Priscilla shot forward and waited to see if she'd have to scream out in pain. She didn't. "Shields asked you to marry him?"

"Yeah."

"Seriously?"

Liz's eyes sparkled. "He did, and I said yes."

Surely she was still dreaming. She wanted to pinch herself to find out for sure, but right now she was pain free and wanted to stay that way.

She rubbed the back of her neck. "How long have I been asleep? Or maybe I was in a coma, because none of this makes any sense to me."

"It's not like that. I mean, we *are* getting married, but not soon. We'd like to get to know each other a little better first."

Priscilla pressed her lips together. Yes. Liz needed to know that Shields was a pauper and he needed to know that she was an escort.

"Neither one of us are traditionalists, so we agreed to the engagement before fully delving into each other's lives. It's backwards, but it works for us."

"You don't know anything about him, Liz."

"I know that I've never met anyone like him in my entire life. I've been with plenty of men and none of them made me smile or made my heart skip a beat."

"It's those other men that I'm worried about. Does Shields know what you do for a living?"

"Did."

"What?"

"What I *did* for a living. I tore up my client list. I haven't "escorted" anyone since the night I met Shields."

Priscilla looked into Liz's eyes. Unflinching blue irises stared back at her. Liz was telling the truth. She'd never been able to tell a lie without her eyes giving her away.

Priscilla had prayed for years for this outcome. She should be ecstatic, but something didn't feel right. Something was off.

"I know I've been out of the loop, and my mind's been a bit fuzzy since the accident, but how long have the two of you been together?"

"Three weeks."

"So not even a month, and you're giving up everything for a man you just met?"

"I'm not giving up everything, just the way I made money. I thought you'd be happy."

"I am." Priscilla tossed the throw covering her to the floor. "It's just that you've always taken forever to make a decision and now you've made a sudden one. I'm just wondering why."

"It's not that sudden. I've been thinking about it for a while now. I just needed a good reason, and now I have one."

Priscilla looked Liz over. She looked more like a soccer mom with her loose jeans and Habakkuk Lions sweatshirt. Completely different from the fashionista she normally looked like. The one who wore designer clothing and expensive jewelry. She still wore a large rock on her right middle finger, but it was the only diamond in sight.

Priscilla scooted to the edge of the recliner and stood. Liz did the same and gently took hold of Priscilla's elbow. When they reached the bathroom door, Liz said, "I'll go in with you."

Priscilla thought about that for a moment. Getting on and off the commode had proven painful in the past, but Barry or her mom had always been there to help her. She needed to get back to her life, to be able to do things on her own. Her back wasn't hurting, and neither was her head. She had to at least try.

"I think I'll be okay. I'll leave the door unlocked in case I need you."

Liz nodded and took a step back.

Priscilla closed the door behind her and used the bathroom without incident. She inched slowly toward the counter. The muscles in her legs were still sore, but way better than they were a few days ago. She washed her hands and leaned against the counter as her head began to spin. She sucked in a deep breath and let it out slowly.

"You okay in there? You want me to come in?"

Liz's voice brought a smile to her face. She craved her independence, but it comforted her knowing a good friend was right outside the door.

"I'm okay. I'll be out in a minute."

She looked in the mirror. Her mom had brushed her hair into a ponytail yesterday morning but had refused to help her apply any make-up. Priscilla had put up a fuss, but her mom insisted she didn't need it. Well, the mirror said she did, and the large bandage on her forehead wasn't helping any.

She grabbed a cloth and washed her face.

The bathroom door swung open. "It's been more than a minute."

"Just washing my face."

Liz walked to the counter and grabbed a brush. "I can brush your hair out if you like."

Priscilla placed the cloth on the counter and walked to the padded bench between the sink and her clawfoot tub.

"I'm worried about you and Shields."

"I know. You think we're moving too fast, and you're afraid of how he'll react when he finds out men paid me money for *services*."

"I'm worried about *you*. You've been head-over-heels since the first night you laid eyes on him, and I just don't want you to get hurt if he's not okay with your past."

Liz laid the brush on the counter. "Do me a favor."

"What?"

"Pray for me."

Priscilla jerked back. "Pray for you? You don't even

believe there's a God."

"I never said that. I said *if* there's a God, I don't like Him very much."

Priscilla started to respond but instead pulled Liz down on the bench next to her. Liz's life had taken a wrong turn long before she was old enough to make decisions on her own. She didn't talk about it much, but Priscilla knew it haunted her. The neglect she'd endured as a child had fueled the way she'd chosen to live her life. And her dislike for God.

"What would you like for me to pray about?"

"Me, my relationship with Shields. It has to work out, Pris. It just has to."

"Why?"

"I'm not going back to my old life. There's nothing left there for me. I'd already made a few steps toward leaving. Meeting Shields just sped up the process. But I don't know who I am anymore. Diamond Liz had a purpose, but Elizabeth Camden is lost. Being with Shields helps me feel less lost. He actually makes me *feel*. But how would I know? I stopped having feelings for people long ago. Sometimes I wonder if I even have a heart."

"Of course you have a heart. If you didn't, you wouldn't be here in this bathroom helping me."

"Here's the thing. I'm messed up emotionally, Pris. Some days I'm riding high and other days I'm crying on my pillow and can't get out of bed. Then Shields would call and everything's blue skies again. He gets me, and he doesn't even fully know me. I need him in my life."

"You never told me you were struggling."

"I wanted to, but I wanted to find out *why* I was struggling first. I'm opening up now, but I still don't know what's wrong with me. That's why I need prayer."

"For understanding?"

She nodded. "And for help. Because if this relationship with Shields goes south, I don't think…"

"Think what?"
"That I'd want to live anymore."

Chapter 10

Priscilla inhaled the scent of the savory soup Mama had set in front of her. The bowl was chock-full of her favorite vegetables. Carrots, green beans, tomatoes, peas, corn, and cabbage. She dipped her spoon in the bowl, blew on it, and opened her mouth wide.

"It's still too hot, Prissy."

"Mama, I'm starving."

Mama pulled a pan of cornbread from the oven and placed it on the stovetop. "I know, but you don't want to burn your tongue either." Mama walked toward her with a piece of cornbread that was just as hot as the still-steaming soup. Priscilla pulled the butter dish toward her and picked out a thick square. She plopped it on the hot bread and licked her lips as she watched it melt.

"Where's that husband of yours?"

Priscilla looked around her. After Liz left, he'd helped her down the stairs to the kitchen, then said he had to return a phone call. That had been about ten minutes ago.

"I don't know." She pushed her chair back to stand. "I'll go find him."

Mama placed a hand on her shoulder. "You'll do no such thing. I don't need you falling down on me." She walked to a wall near the pantry where the intercom was. "Besides, isn't that what this fancy shmancy thing is for?" She pressed the button. "Barry, dinner is ready, and it's hot. Be here in two minutes or you don't eat. No one microwaves my food."

Priscilla dipped her spoon back into the soup and shoved it into her mouth before her mother could protest. It was hot, very hot, but oh, so good.

Mama placed a hand on her hip. "You always have been a rebel."

Priscilla took a bite of the buttery bread and quickly chewed it. "I'm sorry, Mama, but it's been days since I've had an appetite. Now I'm ravenous."

"Take it easy. I don't want you getting sick to your stomach, either."

Barry hurried in and pulled out the chair across from Priscilla. "Mabel, I'm sorry I'm late."

"You're just in time." Mama placed a bowl of soup in front of him, along with a bowl of oyster crackers.

He looked at Priscilla. "That was my attorney. Grantham's been released on bail."

Priscilla almost dropped her spoon. "Released? You mean he's been in jail this whole time?"

Barry nodded.

Mama made her way over to the kitchen sink and leaned her back against it. Her eyes were tight.

Priscilla continued. "Barry, I don't understand. Why wasn't he released the same day? It's not like he has a criminal history, and I'm sure he hired a good lawyer."

"Because he's an idiot."

Priscilla's mouth fell open. She'd never heard Barry call his children a bad name. He disagreed with them plenty, sure. But he'd never called them anything other than the names they were given at birth.

She sighed. "What happened?"

"He tried to bribe one of the arresting officers. When the officer refused, he head-butted the guy."

Priscilla gasped. "You're kidding."

"I wish I was." Barry shook his head. "With the attempted assault against me, damage to my property, and what he did to the officer, I won't be surprised if they throw away the key."

"Who paid his bail? His wife?"

"Definitely not. Margaret's angry at him for putting them in this position. She called a few days ago to apologize for everything that has happened. She said Grantham could rot in jail for all she cared. She rushed off of the phone after that, mumbling something about having to find them a new place to live."

Priscilla groaned. She wasn't surprised Margaret was angry that they'd been kicked out of the mansion. She'd bragged about it all the time as if she and Grantham were the ones who owned it and not Barry. But Margaret wasn't sorry about anything else. Any apology she gave was as fake as her new nose.

Margaret's disdain for Priscilla was just as strong as her husband's. When Grantham had screamed and yelled at her in front of his wife, and everyone else in the store, Margaret had laughed.

Margaret had reached out to her after she'd found out that Priscilla had married Barry. Priscilla had agreed to have lunch with her because she'd thought it'd be a good idea to get to know her new stepson's wife. But all Margaret wanted to talk about was how Priscilla would never be considered part of the family. Five minutes into the luncheon, Priscilla left Margaret sitting at the table. They hadn't spoken to each other since.

Barry swallowed several spoonfuls of soup and pointed to her bowl. "You'll want to eat while it's still hot."

She ate a spoonful, then looked at Mama, who was still

leaning against the sink, except now her arms were crossed.

"You okay, Mama?"

No response.

"Mama?"

She looked at Priscilla. "Yeah?"

"You okay?"

She blinked, then turned back to the counter, where she tossed a salad. She filled up two bowls and placed them in front of Priscilla and Barry.

"Here you go."

Priscilla lifted her fork. "Aren't you going to eat with us?"

"I've got some more prayin' to do."

"But you always eat dinner with us when you're here."

"Something's come up. Something important."

Priscilla slumped her shoulders. Mama had been living with them since the accident, and Priscilla loved having her close. The table had been set for three, so she'd obviously planned on eating with them.

"Mama, please stay and have dinner with us. I was looking forward to it."

Mabel stared at the empty place setting. "Tell you what, how 'bout the two of you enjoy a nice dinner together, and I join you later for dessert." She waved at a covered dish on the counter. "I made a pear cobbler."

Priscilla rounded her eyes and looked at Mama. She turned her lips downward for good measure. It was a face that'd always worked for her as a child, especially when she was trying to get her way.

Mabel kissed the top of her head. "Listen to your husband. Eat before everything gets cold. There's more soup on the stove. I'll be back shortly."

She exited the kitchen, and Priscilla finished her bowl of soup, resisting the urge to tip it and slurp up the remaining broth. She munched on a piece of cornbread and stared at the pitcher of water in the center of the table. Mama hadn't even poured their drinks. She was about to do so before Barry returned from his phone call. Then she'd waited quietly by the sink.

Mama enjoyed dining with them, and as far back as Priscilla could remember, she'd never missed an opportunity to do so, whether she was staying with them for a few days, like she was now, or if she was just visiting. So why did she suddenly change her mind?

"Mabel's been awfully secretive lately."

Priscilla glanced at Barry, then reached for the pitcher. "I know."

"Has she said anything to you about what's bothering her?"

Priscilla lowered her eyes to the table. She didn't want to answer that question. If Mama wanted Barry to know about her concerns, she would've told him. They'd developed an awesome relationship over the years, so why hadn't she clued him in?

She also didn't want to lie to her husband. "Yes, but you know Mama. When she's praying about something, she takes a while to share the details."

"What has she said to you so far?"

Priscilla handed him a glass of water. "I'd rather she tell you. She said she'll join us for dessert, but really, she doesn't have much to go on."

He furrowed his brows. "Go on regarding what?"

She pressed her lips together. She'd said too much.

"Silly?"

"Mama had a vision."

"Okay. That's not unusual for Mabel. What was the vision about?"

Priscilla took a sip of her water.

"Are you going to make me ask twenty questions, or are you going to just tell me?"

"She thinks she knows who did it."

"Did what?"

"Tried to kill me."

His eyes widened. "What?"

"She saw the person who did it in a vision, but she's not going to say who because —"

He pushed away from the table. "Mabel!"

"Barry, please."

"Silly, if she knows who did it, I need to know now. The sooner I get that information to Sgt. Dodge—"

"Please sit down."

He held her gaze. His jaw moved back and forth like it always did when he was thinking. His left foot was pointed toward the entrance that led to the hallway, but Mama was probably not on the main floor anymore. More than likely, she'd climbed the stairs to her bedroom to pray in private. Wherever she was, Barry wanted to head in that direction—it was written all over his face.

"Barry, if you go looking for Mama, you know I'm going to follow you." She thought about playing the injured back card, but she'd been pain-free since she'd awakened earlier. "Besides, if she's in her room and not done praying, she's not going to open her door, anyway."

He dropped into his seat. "The police found the car that hit you abandoned in an industrial parking lot in Corinth. It was registered to a car service in New York, but they'd reported the car stolen months ago. Habakkuk police are still investigating, but it's going nowhere fast. Silly, if your mother knows something—"

"She doesn't know anything. Well, she does, but she doesn't want to say anything until she's sure."

"Did she give you a name?"

"No."

"Anything to go on?"

"Not really. But judging from some things she let slip, I don't think we're dealing with a stranger from out of town. I think it's somebody we know."

Barry ran his hand through his hair. The salt-and-pepper

waves rejected the intrusion and bounced right back into place.

"Silly, ever since Liz called and told me—"

"I know."

His brow furrowed. "You know what?"

"That ever since my accident, you haven't been the same."

He looked at his lap, then back up at her again. "How did you know?"

She smiled. "A wife knows."

He leaned back in the chair. "I haven't been able to work, or sleep … I didn't say anything because I wanted you to focus on getting better, not worrying about me."

"Thanks to you and Mama, I am better. Besides, I was too groggy to worry. I knew what you were going through because I saw pain, worry, and anger every time you looked at me. Your eyes said it all."

"I'm sorry, Silly, but I don't understand it. At first, the police and I thought that I may have been the intended target. With the economy the way it is, King Global isn't as liquid as it once was, and we've had to say no to a lot of deals we've said yes to over the past several years. Without our capital, some of those businesses crumbled. But the idea that someone was after me didn't make sense. You weren't using one of our drivers or even driving my truck. You were driving your car. They had to know it was you."

Priscilla took another sip of water. Everyone in town knew her car. The fact that she had personalized plates that read "Prissy" didn't help. It was also the reason Barry never drove her car.

She was also no stranger to the police. She'd had several run-ins with them in the past. They knew what she used to do for a living, and they were familiar with her former client list. No doubt they were questioned. Barry hadn't said anything, so nothing must have come of it.

Priscilla didn't want to admit it, but when she mentally

scrolled through the list of people who might want her dead, she couldn't help but think of her former "friend" Jacob.

Jacob started off as a client but decided early on that he wanted Priscilla to be exclusive to him. It was an expensive transaction on his behalf, but they'd made it work. For ten years, they made it work. No love, all business. Or at least that's what she'd thought. She'd never loved Jacob, and from the way he'd treated her, she'd assumed the feeling was mutual.

And then she'd met Barry and everything changed.

Jacob was furious, and he let his fists show her how much.

Barry took her in, and they fell in love.

Jacob got his revenge by letting Mama know what kind of daughter she had. Mama had heard rumors, of course, but up until that point, that was all they were to Mama, rumors. But Jacob changed that by showing her proof of Priscilla's lascivious lifestyle.

Priscilla closed her eyes. Tears still formed when she remembered the day she had to tell Mama the truth. It was one of the worst days of her life, having to hurt her mother that way. Especially when she'd had no reason to.

Unlike Liz's parents, Priscilla parents loved her and only wanted the best for her. They were the best parents a girl could've hoped for. She was glad her daddy, a God-fearing man, passed away long before she surrendered to her wayward ways. She missed her Daddy terribly, but there was no way she would've ever been able to look him in the face and tell him about the things she'd done.

She cleared her throat. "Did the police talk to Jacob?"

Barry nodded. "He was at his office when the accident happened. Security footage confirmed it."

Jacob was a criminal defense attorney. The firm he worked for only represented the rich and infamous. She'd met his bosses on several occasions. She was sure they were just as guilty as the clients they represented.

For a while, Jacob did everything he could to convince her to go back to him, including professing his undying love for her to one of Grantham's and Victoria's private investigators.

But a few months after she and Barry married, Jacob invited both of them out for coffee. She'd been hesitant at first, but in the end, she and Barry agreed. Jacob was very cordial and apologized to Priscilla for his behavior. He also wished her the best in her new marriage. He even gave them a wedding gift. A beautifully engraved vase that read Barry & Priscilla and had their wedding date on it.

They'd tossed the vase in the dumpster at the back of the coffee house after Jacob had left. She had no desire to bring anything from her past into her new life with Barry.

They'd thought that'd be the last they heard from him, but a few months ago, she'd started getting text messages from him. Angry messages, which was odd because not only did she ditch her old phone with all of her old contacts, she'd gotten a completely new number, and had taken the security steps to make sure it wasn't listed locally or online. Besides, only a select few had her private number and none of them would've given it to Jacob.

She'd suspected the messages weren't from him. The angry tone was there, but Jacob didn't use swear words. He didn't have to. He had an arrogant way of making you feel like dirt without using them.

"Did you tell the police about the text messages?"

"I did. They took your phone so their tech guys could look into it. They returned it the other day." He nodded toward his office. "It's in there charging. Your suspicions were right. Those calls didn't come from Jacob's phone. They said his number was spoofed."

Priscilla scratched her head. "Then I'm lost on who would want to harm me. Not all of my previous client relationships ended well, but none of them ended in such a way that they'd want me dead. Not to mention risk bringing unwanted attention to their extra-curricular activities."

Mama walked into the kitchen. "Prissy, keep that kind of talk away from the dinner table."

Priscilla winced. "We were just discussing—"

"I know what you were discussin'."

Barry leaned forward. "Mabel, who tried to run my wife off the road?"

Mama went to a drawer and pulled out a pie server. "I don't know who was behind the wheel of that car, but I'm pretty sure I know who put the driver up to it."

He turned his chair toward her. "Who?"

"I can't say, not yet."

"Mab—"

"Patience, Barry. Trust me, you don't want me to rush this."

He scoffed. "Patience?"

Mama put a hand on her hip. "I want to catch the people who tried to kill my daughter as much as you do. But if I mention a name to the police before I'm sure and I'm wrong, then what? A lot of people close to us would be hurt and a family ripped to shreds for no reason."

Priscilla exchanged glances with Barry before he continued. "Are you saying that whoever did this is close to us?"

Mama turned and lifted the cover off the cobbler. "I've said too much."

"You haven't said *much* of anything."

Mama walked toward him with the pie slicer pointed in his direction. "I've said what I've said, and that's that. When I know more, you'll know more. Got it?"

"Just tell the police who you suspect."

"You can ask the police to question me if you want, but I'm not going to tell them any more than I've told you."

Barry threw his hands in the air and turned to look out the large picture window surrounding the kitchen table.

Mama laid the slicer on the table and placed a hand on

Barry's shoulder. "You know Edith and I were good friends, right?"

He whipped around. "What has my late wife got to do with this?"

"Answer my question."

His nostrils flared. "I do know that. Edith loved you and trusted you. But what has that got to do with—"

"Was she a good judge of character?"

"Of course. She was the best."

"I need you to trust me like she did."

"Mabel, I do trust you." He blew out a breath. "It's just that—"

"You want answers. Trust God and trust me to trust Him, and you'll get them."

Barry looked at Priscilla, and she nodded. He wanted answers and so did she, but Mama was right—God would provide the answers in time.

Mama picked up the pie slicer and returned to the cobbler. She cut it, then pulled three dessert plates out of the cabinet above her and placed them on the granite counter.

Her movements were slow and careful, just like the words she'd chosen to speak to Barry earlier.

But *why* was Mama being so careful? And whose family could be torn apart?

Priscilla stared at the floor. It didn't give her any answers, but it did spark another question.

What did the late Edith King have to do with any of this?

Chapter 11

Liz stopped walking and turned to Priscilla. "What? You can't be serious."

Priscilla wrapped her scarf around her tighter. Barry and Mama had been hesitant about letting her outside of the house, but the doctor convinced them that fresh air was good medicine, and he was right. She was cold, but she felt better than she had in days. Technically, it was still fall, but the frigid morning air hinted that winter wasn't far off.

"I'm serious. Liz, I'm worried about you."

"I know, and you're a good friend. But there's no way I can stay here at the estate with you."

"Why not?"

"You and Barry have been married a few years, but I still consider the two of you newlyweds. And besides, you already have one house guest. Mabel's not leaving your side until this whole thing with the accident is resolved and who knows when that'll be."

"You know as well as I do how many rooms we have in this house. Barry and I could go days without seeing you or Mama if we wanted to. You'll still have your privacy, but

I'd like for you to be close and not way across town in that lonely high-rise."

Liz giggled. "Well, I'm not exactly alone there. Shields stops by every evening after work."

"That's different. He's your boyfriend."

"Fiance."

Priscilla had intentionally left out that part, and she'd rather not talk about Shields at all. He was a nice guy, and she hoped in the end things would work out for them. But the last time she'd spoken to her friend, she'd talked about not wanting to live if things didn't go well between her and Shields. Liz needed her and Priscilla doubted her friend's depressed state had anything to do with the success or failure of her relationship.

"Whatever. It's not the same as having your best friend to talk to. And besides, if you stay here, he wouldn't have to drive so far to see you."

Liz stepped in front of Priscilla. "What is this really about?"

"What do you mean?"

"*You're* suggesting I move closer to Shields? You don't see something wrong with that?"

Priscilla saw a *lot* wrong with that. But she couldn't go stay with Liz. Barry would never agree to it. Except for the scar on her forehead, most of her injuries had healed, but Liz lived in downtown Habakkuk in a luxury suite. Too many people. Until the authorities knew more, Barry wanted her to stay close to home, where they had security.

And she wanted to keep Liz close to gauge her emotional state. Barry would balk at Liz staying so close to Shields because he wouldn't want him distracted. Shields was one of his best workers, and no doubt having Liz a few feet away could cause problems.

"Have you and Shields been intimate with each other?"

Liz shrugged. "We've snuggled and watched movies together. Fully clothed. That's been the extent of our intimacy."

Priscilla smiled at Liz. "Good. Then I won't have to fight that battle."

"You mean the one where you'll have to make sure Barry doesn't find Shields and me alone in a barn somewhere?"

"Yep. That one."

Liz chuckled. "It doesn't matter. I know you want to keep a closer eye on me, and I'd be lying if I said I didn't need it. But I can't stay with you and Barry, Pris. He's got his son's legal issues and your safety to deal with. I'm not going to put a strain on your marriage like that."

Priscilla shoved her hands in her jacket pockets. "Fine. What about Penelope?"

"Your sister, Penelope? What about her?"

"She's state-side again." Priscilla's sister and brother-in-law were part of a ministry that spent six months a year treating patients in underdeveloped countries. "Their apartment isn't far from yours. She'd love the company."

"What about her husband?"

"Still overseas. She works at her private practice when she's here, but that's also downtown, near you. As a matter of fact, Mama told me the other day that her administrative assistant is on maternity leave, and she's looking for someone to fill in. Mostly answering phone calls and scheduling appointments. You can do that. And it'll also keep your mind busy."

"I've never worked in an office setting, Priscilla. You know that."

"You'll do fine. Her assistant has seven kids, so I've filled in for her before. Penelope has a software program that does all the work. All you have to do is type in the patient's name and all of their medical information comes up. You're pretty good with computers, so you'll get the hang of it in no time. And you're good with people. It'll work."

"I don't know, Pris."

"It's not like you'll be working for a stranger. You've known Penny just as long as you've known me. And she's super easy to work for. Mostly."

"Mostly?"

"She's a real stickler for time. When she says be there at eight, she really means seven."

The wind picked up and Liz pulled her fur-lined cap over her ears. "I can't believe I'm actually considering this."

"It'll work out great. She's lonely in that big apartment without her husband here, and she needs help at the office. You've said you feel lost since you're not working anymore. Wouldn't you feel better volunteering than weeping at home alone in your bed?"

"Wait. Volunteering?"

Priscilla feigned surprise. "Oh, did I forget to mention that part?"

Liz crossed her arms. "Yeah."

"Both her assistant and her assistant's spouse work there for free. He takes care of anything that needs fixing, cleaning, or repairing. In return, Penelope provides medical care for the entire family."

"Sweet deal. But I don't need medical services." She kicked at the grass with her boot. "At least not for my body, anyway."

"She also has a degree in psychology."

Liz looked up. "I forgot about that."

"Yeah, she's the wonder child Mama always brags about."

"Mabel loves you."

"I know. But that doesn't mean she's proud of me."

"Let's not go there, Pris."

"Go where?"

Liz stepped toward her. "The whole, 'I'm not Mama's favorite' thing. I don't want to hear it."

"I was only saying that—"

"Did Mabel ever chain you to an iron pole in the

basement because you asked for something to eat?

"No, of course not. What I was trying to say was—"

"That you were thrown outside naked in below-freezing weather because you asked for a blanket?"

"No."

"Then shut up."

Priscilla looked into her friend's eyes. There was no anger there, only hurt. And confirmation that she was right. Liz's depression had little to do with her walking away from her profession and a lot to do with her past.

She clasped Liz's hands in hers. "I'm so sorry. I wasn't thinking."

Liz pulled her hands away and wiped at her eyes. "No. I'm the one who needs to apologize. I have no idea where all of that came from."

They walked to a nearby firepit that was surrounded by boulders and wooden benches. It was too early to start a fire and the benches would be freezing, but she needed to sit and talk with Liz. Mama and Barry were still inside the house, and so were several staff members. She needed privacy if she was ever going to get Liz to open up.

She sat on one of the benches and Liz sat across from her, the firepit between them. Priscilla wanted to start the conversation, but Liz's focus was on the sky. She stared at it and kept shaking her head. After a few minutes, she looked at Pris.

"Yesterday, I spent most of the morning scrolling through social media. Lola had shared a video of a family doing things for each other. A young child plucking flowers from the garden for his mom. A wife surprising her husband at work with his favorite lunch … you know, cheesy stuff like that." She blinked away tears. "But the video got to me, you know? I didn't have that type of family growing up. No one ever did anything kind. Ever. My parents weren't kind to each other, and they definitely weren't kind to me."

Priscilla had seen the video that Lola had shared. It was

about not taking for granted the people closest to you. It was a heartwarming video and Priscilla had smiled as she'd watched it. But it sounded like for Liz, it was a stark reminder of something she'd longed for, but never received.

"Pris, I know you think I haven't known Shields long enough to be as emotionally attached to him as I am, but he does those things for me. Everything from flowers to making sure my garbage cans are ready for pickup. I've never asked him to do any of those things. And all I'm able to give him in return are mood swings and unpredictable crying. But he does them anyway, and my heart melts every time."

"Sometimes it's the little things that mean a lot."

She nodded. "One night, my parents took turns beating me with an extension cord. When they were done, they threw me down the stairs into the basement. My back and legs were bleeding, and I was in so much pain. I didn't dare cry out because if they heard me, that would've made things worse. The basement was so dark, but somehow a sliver of moonlight had made its way through a crack in the foundation. I felt so alone. My parents didn't let me go to school, so I had no friends, no siblings, or any other family that I knew about."

She zipped her jacket up tighter. "But all of a sudden I saw this mouse. I guess it had made its way through the same cracks the moonlight did, and he scurried toward me. I'd shoo him away, but he always kept coming back. He'd climb on my lap and sit. Just sit, like he knew I needed the company. Then he shot off my lap, disappeared into the basement, and came back with a peanut butter cracker and wanted me to take it. I hadn't had food in days, and I was so tempted to eat it, but I didn't. I let him enjoy it. My mom used crackers in the traps, but somehow he'd managed to get the cracker away from it and brought it to me. He'd risked his life. For *me*. I've never forgotten that. It was the only kindness I'd ever been shown in that house."

"I'm sorry you had to go through that."

"Don't be. Henry was nice. We were friends for years."

Priscilla hiked a brow. "Henry?"

"The mouse."

Priscilla hated rodents, but for some strange reason, she wished she'd gotten the chance to know Henry.

"Does Shields know about Henry?"

Liz shook her head. "If I tell him about Henry, then I'd have to tell him the story behind it. And that'll lead to questions I'm not ready to answer."

Priscilla shoved her hands into her pockets. This was the first time she'd heard about Henry, and Liz hadn't talked this much about her parents in over a decade. And even then, she'd said very little. Priscilla and Liz were the same age, so what little she knew about Liz's childhood, she'd learned from Mama.

Black and white pictures of a malnourished Liz being carried from her home by a social worker made the front page of local newspapers for weeks. Her parents were arrested, but what happened to them after that no one knew. They never returned to Habakkuk, and if Liz knew where they were now, she'd never said anything about that either.

She'd said a lot about other things, though. She'd talked with Priscilla about everything else—from the mundane to the most intimate. But her childhood? She kept that close to the vest. And her years spent with the supposed relative after she'd been taken from her parents? She was even more tight-lipped about that. Priscilla often wondered what had happened to Liz during those years. Was it trauma that stopped her from talking about it? Or something else?

"Hey, would you ladies like for me to start a fire for you? Because it looks like the two of you are freezing."

Priscilla looked to her left. Shields was walking toward them. She waved.

He nodded, but his focus was on Liz. He quickened his steps and sat next to her on the bench. "You okay?"

She wiped at her eyes and tried to smile. When that

failed, she said, "No." Then covered her face with her hands and sobbed.

Shields pulled off his work gloves and nudged Liz closer to him. She laid her head on his shoulders. He wrapped an arm around her waist.

Priscilla glanced up at the house. If Barry looked out one of the kitchen windows, he'd see Shields sitting with them, hugging Liz, and whispering in her ear.

He'd also see that Shields wasn't working. He was, after all, on the clock.

Both Barry and her sister had strong opinions about one's personal life interfering with the job. Priscilla would be able to smooth this one over with Barry, maybe even to the point of asking him to not be too hard on Shields. But it was clear that her idea of Liz temporarily living with them wouldn't work. But it had led to the conversation of Liz living and working with Penelope, and that was a good thing. Penelope could help Liz in ways she couldn't.

Her cell phone rang. She pulled her phone from her jacket pocket. It was Barry.

She tapped the phone on. "Hi, honey."

"Let me speak to Shields."

She looked over at Shields. He was brushing a wisp of hair from Liz's cheek.

Liz needed Shields by her side right now and Priscilla didn't want to interrupt them. "Okay, I'm on my way."

"What?"

"I'm on my way."

He let out a low groan. "I know what you're doing."

"Maybe later then?"

"No. I need to talk to him now. I've tried calling his phone and one of the other hands answered. He left his phone in the stable, along with several unfinished jobs. I know he's there with you and Liz, I can see the three of you from here."

"Kinda busy."

"I know he is, and it doesn't matter. I could walk over

there, but I don't want to embarrass him. I just want you to give him the phone."

Priscilla covered the mouthpiece with her hand. "I'm sorry guys, I have to go. Liz, I'll call you after I talk to Penelope, okay?"

Liz nodded and snuggled closer to Shields.

Priscilla stood and walked toward the horse barn. "Where are you?"

"Why are you walking to me and not Shields?"

Barry was in the barn. Hopefully, she'd be able to talk with him privately for a few minutes.

"Because I want a hug." Which was true. She loved hugs from her husband, but of course, her main reason was to talk to him before he talked to Shields.

"If you think you're going to be able to distract me from—"

"Oh, we both know I'll be able to distract you."

He chuckled.

"But I'd also like to talk to you about something."

"Does it have to do with you or Shields?"

"Liz. But that would include Shields too, so yes, it's about him."

She was within a few feet of Barry now, so she turned her phone off and slid it back into her pocket.

Barry walked up to her and gave her a hug. "What's going on?"

She hesitated to step out of the warm embrace, but she wanted to look into his eyes when she talked to him.

"Liz is not in a good place."

"What do you mean?"

"Mentally. Emotionally. She hasn't been herself for weeks now. I'm afraid for her, Barry."

"Afraid? For Liz?"

"Yes. Something's not right."

"As in?"

"As in, I don't think it's safe for her to be alone."

Barry took a step back. "Safe? Are you saying she's—"

"I'm saying she's said some things that have me concerned."

He looked over Priscilla's shoulder. "Shields is still sitting at the firepit with her, but I'm not sure how he fits into this. Do you think he's causing her to feel that way?"

"No, it's the opposite. He's good for her. He comforts her."

He furrowed his brows.

"Not that kind of comfort. But it's the type of comfort Lola and I aren't able to give her. She needs lots of attention right now. The good kind, not the kind she'd sought out before."

"Still, if you're afraid for her, she needs professional help, not Shields."

"I know, and she's agreed to meet with Penelope. I'm going to call her after I'm finished talking with you. But until then, I was wondering if I could ask a favor?"

He looked down at her. "Sure."

"Can Shields have the rest of the day off?"

"What? No."

She lowered her eyes. "Okay." Taking the path of least resistance worked wonders in getting Barry to see things her way.

He rubbed a hand across the back of his neck. "Why should he have the day off?"

"Because Penelope's working, Ram and Lola are out of town, and you won't let me stay with her at her apartment."

"It's not safe for you to do that yet, Silly. Someone tried to kill you."

"That's my point. I can't stay with her and I don't know when Penelope will meet up with her, but until we get that worked out, I think Shields is the perfect person to keep an eye on her. Please, Barry? She doesn't have any family, well, none that I know of anyway. The last thing she needs right now is to be alone."

He scratched at his cheek. "Fine. But let me talk to him first."

"Please don't be too hard on him. He was just trying to help us, but then Liz started crying and—"

"I don't want to talk to him about that. I want to talk to him about his Christian walk."

Priscilla leaned back. "Shields is a Christian?"

"As of last week, he is. He stayed late last Saturday and asked if I could help him understand some things he'd read in the Bible. But in the end, yeah, he asked what he needed to do to be saved, and we walked through it together."

"Barry, that's wonderful." She tilted her head to the side. "Am I right in assuming your talk with him will be about avoiding temptation?"

"You assume correctly."

She hugged her husband again. She was glad Shields had someone like Barry in his life. She was glad that *she* had someone like Barry in her life. He was rough around the edges, but it all stemmed from a good place. He had a heart of gold.

And so did her sister.

Priscilla didn't know if she'd ever get over being jealous of Penelope. She wasn't jealous of her sister's successes, she was jealous of her relationship with their mother. Mama beamed whenever Penelope was around. Mama was so proud of her oldest daughter.

Priscilla still picked fights with her sister over the tiniest of things, but none of that ever mattered to Penelope. Whenever Priscilla needed her, she was always right there. Even if she had to fly over a couple of continents to do so.

And now she needed her sister again.

She kissed Barry, retrieved her phone from her pocket, and dialed her sister.

Chapter 12

After her conversation with Penelope, Priscilla strode to her favorite place on the estate—Peace Hill.

Their home was situated on thirty acres of land in one of the most coveted communities in Habakkuk, known as Habakkuk Hills. Habakkuk itself was founded over a hundred years ago, and according to the Habakkuk Historical Society, the town was named after the Old Testament prophet.

There were only seven homes in Habakkuk Hills, and Barry's estate was undoubtedly the largest. Priscilla shook her head. *Their* estate. They'd been married over three years, and she still had a hard time believing, let alone voicing, even internally, that this was her home as well. Every bit of it. Barry and his legal team had made sure that there were no loopholes in any of the documents. He wanted her to inherit this property and left several of the others to be divided up between his children and grandchildren. But *this* property, and everything in it and on it, would belong to her.

Habakkuk was located in the heart of the Ozark Mountains in southwestern Missouri, sandwiched between two tourist towns and miles from the nearest city. Habakkuk Hills was nestled in north Habakkuk and backed to the White River.

The town was surrounded by mountains, bluffs, and rolling hills, and Habakkuk Hills was no exception.

When she reached Peace Hill, one of the highest points on the estate, she stopped and listened, ready to respond to any creature who was eager to chat.

Barry had purchased the property long before he'd met Priscilla, but Peace Hill was one of the reasons he knew he had to have it.

She'd visited the hill over a hundred times, and the scene never failed to take her breath away. From here, she could see the house, the circular drive and oak trees in front of it, the barns, stables, arenas, gazebos, pool house, and alfalfa fields. When she faced the opposite direction, she was surrounded by the beauty of the mountains and the sound of the river. And if she'd brought her binoculars, she'd be able to get a glimpse of the wildlife that made their home in Mark Twain National Forest, which had riding trails that bordered the property and led into the park.

Priscilla leaned her head back and inhaled the frigid air. Her nose didn't appreciate it, but she didn't care. She'd been cooped up for weeks and now that she was strong enough to walk the property, she wanted to take advantage of every moment before Mama or Barry ordered her back inside.

Mama would fuss about not wanting her to catch a cold and Barry would say that she was doing too much too soon. She didn't mind the mothering or the protectiveness. In fact, she craved it. There was a time when, like Liz, she'd felt alone. She'd been too embarrassed to tell Mama or her sister what she'd been up to, and there wasn't a man in the entire Midwest who'd cared about her mental well-being.

What a miserable life she'd led, but she'd been too blinded by the fruits of her sins to do anything about it. And if it hadn't been for the grace of God, she'd still be miserable.

Worse than that—she'd be lonely—and that was an entirely different kind of misery.

Now she had the life she'd always wanted. A wonderful relationship with Mama, a man who loved her, and friends that cared about her. Barry's wealth was a blessing, but it wasn't a necessity.

Five years ago, she never could've imagined saying those words, but it was true. She remembered the stories Mama used to tell about how hard it was for her and Daddy in the decades leading up to the civil rights era. Jobs were available, but not always to them. Making ends meet to keep a roof over their head and food on the table for their two daughters had been a struggle. But she'd emphasized that just because they were broke, it didn't mean that they were broken. They'd worked hard—even at jobs they despised— but they'd also loved, laughed, and danced like they didn't have a care in the world. Because, according to Mama, God had been in the middle of the struggle with them, and He'd made sure all of their needs were met. And those needs also included love, joy, and laughter.

Both of her parents had been strict disciplinarians, but the bulk of Priscilla's childhood memories were full of the light-heartedness that had permeated their home.

She wished she'd been able to meet Barry when she was younger. She longed to give him a child. She wouldn't have been able to give birth to one, but they could've adopted. However, those days were long gone.

Yet she still desired to make their home a happy one. Full of the love and laughter Mama talked about so often. Barry's wealth made that easier, but if he lost everything he owned, including everything at the bottom of the hill, she'd still be happy, and she'd make it her mission to make sure that he was happy, too. Even if that meant living in a cardboard box.

But living was hard when someone wanted you dead.

Whoever ran her car off the road had hoped she

wouldn't survive, but God had other plans.

She didn't know what those plans were, but apparently, they didn't include her death. Not yet, anyway.

She heard a noise and turned to look down at the house. Lydia's car and Victoria's were now parked in the circular drive. Lydia went inside the house and Victoria walked toward her dad, who was grooming Rich Brown outside of the tack barn.

Priscilla regretted not having her earbuds. When Liz called to come over, Priscilla had been listening to her friend Eve's latest praise and worship album. She'd meant to grab the earbuds before she'd stepped outside to meet Liz. If she'd had them, she would've been listening to the rest of Eve's music while taking in the beauty around her, and she never would've heard the arrival of Barry's daughter.

Victoria would eventually ask where Priscilla was, but she hoped Barry wouldn't tell her. No one could ruin a peaceful moment like Victoria.

Priscilla returned to her view and climbed a few steps higher before settling on the leaf-covered ground.

She pulled on her gloves and removed the scarf from around her neck. She opened it wide and wrapped it around her head and ears as well. There was only a slight breeze, but it was a cold one, and it had started giving her a headache.

She closed her eyes and listened to the rippling sounds of the White River. She remembered the first time she'd gone fishing in that river. It was with Barry, and he'd wanted to teach her how to catch rainbow trout. She'd frolicked with him more than she'd fished, but she could almost still smell the aromas from their kitchen as Mama and Chef Rigalta worked their magic.

She didn't know if trout were still in the river or not, but when she headed back down the hill, she'd ask Barry to take her fishing again. Not for her sake—she didn't like touching fishing poles, let alone bait—but because it would make Barry happy. He'd told her he found it relaxing, and with everything going on between him and his kids, and especially after Victoria's spontaneous visit today, he'd more than likely need cheering up.

She zipped her jacket tighter and was about to start a prayer when her phone vibrated. It was Mama. Priscilla sighed. She didn't want to answer, but if she didn't, Mama would come looking for her. Mama was in excellent shape and climbing the hill wouldn't be a problem for her. But there were several tricky rock formations that, if stepped on the wrong way, could send her tumbling down the hill. Mama was spry, but she wasn't young. Recovering from a fall like that wouldn't be easy.

Priscilla pressed the talk button. "Hi, Mama."

"Liz left with Shields a while ago. Where are you?"

"I wanted to continue stretching my legs for a bit, so I went for a walk. I'm still on the property, at the top of Peace Hill. Barry knows I'm here."

"Can you come back to the house?"

"In a little while, sure."

"I meant now."

"Why?"

There was a long pause before Mama answered. "I don't know … I think I'd just feel better if you were where I could see you."

Priscilla opened her mouth to protest, then closed it. Mama was one of the first people to see her after the accident, and receiving that phone call from Liz couldn't have been easy. Of course, her mother wanted to keep an eye on her. If she had kids, she'd probably want to do the same. At least, until after whoever was responsible was caught. But there was something else. Mama didn't use words like, '*I don't know*', or '*I think*'. She was decisive with her thoughts and didn't have qualms about voicing them.

Priscilla stood and wiped off her jeans. "Sure, Mama. I'll head down the hill now. Is Lydia still there?"

"No, and she told me to tell you she's sorry she missed

you. She'll be back tomorrow morning."

"Okay. Mama?"

"Yes?"

"What's the *real* reason you want me back at the house?"

Another long pause.

And another.

Priscilla looked at her phone. The call was still connected. "Mama, you there?"

"I'm here. Just come home, okay?"

Priscilla agreed and tapped the phone off.

What in the world had Mama so nervous?

Chapter 13

Priscilla neared the bottom of the hill and saw Victoria waiting for her.

"Hi, Victoria."

Victoria took a step forward and attempted what Priscilla assumed to be a smile.

"Daddy said you were up there on Peace Hill."

"I was."

Victoria's blue eyes darkened. Barry had dark brown eyes, but Victoria's mother's eyes had been blue. Priscilla had always thought the darker color would've suited her better. Her soul was as dark as the hair bound into a tight bun on top of her head.

Victoria pointed at the hills behind Priscilla. "Did you know that if you took a right at that large boulder there, it'd take you to a spot higher than Peace Hill?"

Priscilla didn't have to turn around to know which boulder Victoria was referring to. She'd passed it a million times on her trips up and down the hill. However, she didn't know there was a higher hill.

"I didn't know that. I'll check it out the next time I go

up."

Victoria started up the hill. "We could go now if you'd like. I know the way. We used to go up there all the time with Daddy when we were kids."

They did? Why hadn't Barry told her about that spot?

"No thanks. Maybe another time."

"You sure? I think you'd love it. Peace Hill pales in comparison to Bad Man's Slope. There's even a natural waterfall."

"Bad Man's what?"

Victoria waved her hand. "That's just the name Grantham and I gave it when we were kids." She continued up the hill. "Coming?"

Victoria had piqued her interest. Any other day, she might've tagged along, but Mama was waiting for her.

"No, but I'm glad you mentioned it. I'll have Barry show it to me later."

Victoria shook her head and snickered.

Priscilla folded her arms across her chest. "What?"

"Why does Daddy want you to inherit a property you know nothing about?"

"That's a question for your father, not me."

Victoria picked up a rock and tossed it before looking up the hill. "You know who did know everything about this property? My mother. She loved this place." Victoria snapped her gaze back to Priscilla. "The fact that Daddy's giving it to a seductress and not his children has Mother turning over in her grave." Victoria walked back down the hill, her arm extended, and her finger pointed at Priscilla's nose. "*You're* the reason my mother's not able to rest in peace."

What in the world was this woman talking about?

"And by the way, she hates what you've done to her home."

"Who hates it?"

"My mother."

Priscilla blinked. "You've … talked with your mother?"

"Don't look at me like that." She picked up another rock. "I know my mother's dead. I have a friend who communicates with the other side, so yes, I've talked to her."

Priscilla pressed her lips together. Edith passed away over ten years ago. Barry had told her that Victoria still grieved her passing, but trying to communicate with her? No way would Barry have left out that detail.

"Have you talked with your dad about this?"

"About talking with Mom?" she chuckled. "No. With his crazy Christian beliefs? He'd probably send an exorcist to my house."

"Your dad's not Catholic, so he wouldn't do that. But I do think you should tell him."

"Not a chance." She rolled the tennis ball-sized rock around in her hand. "Well, if you're not going to let me show you the slope, I'm done here. Just wanted you to see what a *really* good view looks like."

"I'm good."

Victoria stared at her for several seconds before dropping the rock and making her way to the front of the house.

Priscilla shoved her hands in her pockets. Was Victoria just a daughter still grieving the loss of her mother?

Or was she bat crazy?

Either way, Barry needed to know about their conversation.

She just hoped it wasn't too late.

Chapter 14

Priscilla plopped down on the leather sofa in front of the fireplace.

After they'd married, Barry had offered to move and purchase a home for them elsewhere. He loved this home but understood why Priscilla might not. He'd brought his first wife here, and together they'd raised their children in this house.

But Priscilla couldn't ask him to move. She, more than anyone, knew how much this place meant to him. It was the first piece of land he'd purchased as a developer. He didn't have the money then to build it out the way he'd wanted, so for years it sat untouched. Then, little by little and with lots of blood, sweat, and tears, he was able to develop a large part of it with the help of friends and neighbors.

The more successful he became, the more he was able to add to it. But it wasn't just the house or the land that it sat on, it was everything surrounding it that Barry loved. And no matter how hard they'd searched Habakkuk and the towns around it, they simply couldn't find anything else that came close to what he'd had here.

So she'd decided to make this her home. Barry had some concerns but was relieved when she'd agreed to make the home more to her liking, which she did.

The room she was in now was previously Barry's and Edith's bedroom and had taken up a fourth of the main floor. Priscilla didn't want to intrude on Barry's memories with his late wife, so she combined two of the eight rooms upstairs into a new master bedroom. Then she'd asked her decorator to turn this room into a gathering area for friends and family.

The two-story brick fireplace was new, and so was the loft above it. Priscilla had picked out the furniture with care. She wanted everyone to feel welcome when they entered this room. It was large enough for her to accommodate a variety of styles and preferences. There was leather furniture, as well as upholstered, iron, and wood. The decorator had also given the room a warm, rustic look while still allowing it to have a traditional feel.

She looked into the fireplace and was glad Barry had started a fire. The weather was getting nippier by the second, and the weatherman had mentioned the possibility of snow. That would be nice, but she'd rather the snow waited until the winter months. True, they were only weeks away from that, but snow in the fall was too soon. She liked it when every season had a chance to show off its own unique splendor before the next one arrived.

Her life with Barry was like that. She'd had no previous love in her life, but Barry had. He'd been married to the love of his life for almost forty years. And they'd had a great life together before Edith's season ended, and she slipped into eternity.

Priscilla took in the surrounding décor. It had been quite the ordeal, but somehow she'd managed to redecorate the entire house, and even tear down and put up a few walls without completely eliminating Edith's touches from it. Even though she and Barry had entered into a new season of their own, she still wanted Edith's children and grandchildren to see glimpses of their mother and grandmother when they came to visit.

But they rarely did.

Every birthday and holiday, Priscilla had invited them over. Sometimes they'd come, but when they did, they'd talk to Barry only and ignore her. She'd been okay with that because he was the one they'd come to see, anyway. Her goal had been to make their visits as pleasant as possible.

They'd never thanked her, and if Barry wasn't around, they'd scurry off without saying goodbye. But not once had she ever thought about asking them to stop visiting.

Until today.

Victoria's visit had taken things to another level.

Priscilla hadn't been on board with Barry banning Grantham from the estate, but Grantham wasn't her son, so she stood by what Barry'd thought best.

She'd hoped it would only last a few days, but it had been weeks. Barry didn't talk about the situation with Grantham much, but he didn't have to. The pain was etched into the lines of his face.

And now she had to ask him to do the same with his daughter.

Priscilla removed her gloves, scarf, and jacket, and tossed them on the leather bench next to her.

Mama had brewed a fresh pot of coffee and had given Priscilla a cup when she'd returned. It had warmed her some, but not nearly enough.

She went to sit on the hearth.

The heat made its way through her thinly knitted sweater and banished the lingering cold from her body.

Victoria's face flashed before her, and she wondered what it would take to thaw the coldness in the woman's veins.

Priscilla pulled out her phone. She'd sent Barry a text earlier and asked him to meet her here. He'd responded with a thumbs up over thirty minutes ago. Where was he?

He needed to know what Victoria had said regarding Edith. Priscilla didn't care that Victoria *thought* she was talking with her mother. It was the fact that she was keeping company with people who practiced dark arts that concerned her.

What Victoria was involved in was ungodly, and Priscilla wanted no part of it.

The fire crackled beside her, and she looked into the flames. *Lord, Victoria needs you. She's hurting and broken, Lord, and headed down a dangerous road. Rescue her, Lord.*

The thump of boots against wooden planks caught her attention. Barry walked in and laid his Stetson and jacket on the bench. He rubbed his hands together and joined her on the hearth. "I can't believe how fast the temperature's dropping."

"I was thinking the same thing earlier."

He raked a hand through his hair and loosened the top button of his shirt. "What did you want to talk to me about?"

Priscilla bowed her head. "I had a conversation with Victoria earlier."

He nodded. "She told me she was going to say hi to you on her way out."

"She said a lot more than *hi*."

"What do you mean?"

"I think Victoria's using a medium to communicate with her mom."

His head jerked back. "What on earth would make you think that?"

She blew out a breath. "Actually, I don't think it. I *know* that's what she's doing. She told me she has a friend who's been helping her speak to Edith."

He scrubbed a hand across his face and stared straight ahead.

She scooted closer to him and gently rubbed his back. "I'm sorry, Barry. But I knew you'd want to know."

He stood. "Give me a minute, okay?" He walked over to his hat and coat.

"Where are you going?"

"For a walk, I'll be back soon."

The kitchen door closed and she dropped her head into her hands. Did she do the right thing? Should she have waited? No. Barry would want to know immediately what Victoria was involved in, but the timing couldn't have been worse. She blinked away tears. He was hurting. It was hard enough having one child causing grief, but two? His *only* two?

She lifted a hand to her neck and gently fingered the diamond-accented emerald necklace Barry had given her shortly before they were married. Besides her wedding ring, it was the only piece of fine jewelry she wore anymore. This was the necklace that had let her know, without a shadow of a doubt, that she was in love. Not because of the expensive jewel—she'd had plenty of those from lustful men with lascivious intentions—but because of the heart in the man who gave it. That was the day she'd learned that there was a big difference between glitter and gold.

She stood and grabbed her jacket and gloves. Her husband didn't need to be alone right now.

She exited through the kitchen, walked down the back steps, and headed to the far west side of the grounds. She continued past the barns, arenas, and outbuildings, to where there was nothing but an old historic windmill, and a patch of flat land surrounded by coppery big bluestem—a native grass that grew close to four feet tall.

When she needed time to think, she climbed up to Peace Hill. When Barry wanted to be alone, he came here.

She didn't find him in his usual position—sitting on top of a bale of hay, arms folded, staring across copper and golden grasses—so she walked further behind the windmill and stopped. Barry was on the ground, flat on his back, and staring at the sky with his arms stretched out at his sides.

Her heart raced. She wanted to run to him, to see if he'd fallen or injured himself, but he wasn't writhing in agony or struggling to get up. And he was alive. His lips were moving and there was slight movement in his legs.

It looked as though he'd intentionally laid down there.

She remained where she was until her heart rate slowed. When it did, she walked quietly toward him.

"Barry?"

He continued to look at the sky. "I'm okay."

"I know." She knelt beside him. "But I am wondering why you're laying on the ground like this."

"Surrendering."

"I don't understand."

"Surrendering to God. All of it. Everything. The people who tried to kill you. Grantham. Victoria. My anger and frustration. Disappointment. I'm trying to surrender it all."

She clasped his hand.

He continued. "This morning, the police thought they had a lead on who rented the vehicle that hit you. This afternoon, they called back and said it was another dead end. Then I found out Grantham is looking at serious prison time for head-butting the cop who arrested him. Then when you told me Victoria was—"

She kissed his hand. "I'm sorry, Barry. I didn't know. I should've waited, I should've—"

"You did what you should've done. She's my daughter. I needed to know."

Priscilla gripped his hand tighter.

He shook his head. "You shouldn't have come, Silly. Your body is still healing. You don't need the burden of all of this."

"Then why I am here?"

"In the field?"

"No. Why am I here *here*?"

"What do you mean?"

"I'm your wife. We're supposed to be together in this.

Three years ago, you asked me to share life with you, and I made a vow to do so. In the good times and the bad. I just need for you to let me."

He looked at her. "I *need* you to get better. I can't lose you."

"I'm getting stronger every day, Barry. I'm not going anywhere."

He smiled, and she nodded up at the sky. "Are you done?"

"With what? Surrendering?"

"Yeah."

He groaned. "Not even close. I want to hurt the men who hurt you. Part of me hopes they'll show up here on the property so I can blow a hole the size of Texas through their hearts with Betsy."

Betsy was his beloved Remington rifle.

"And the *casting my cares part* has been difficult. I seem determined to keep holding on to them."

She let go of his hand and stretched out beside him.

"What are you doing?"

"Surrendering with you."

"Why?"

"Because I love you."

He pulled her closer and wrapped his right arm around her waist. The windmill creaked and skreighed above them as a cold gust of wind blew across the field.

As the wind picked up, so did her hope in God's faithfulness and power.

Barry prayed quietly beside her while the heat from his body warmed her.

If her assailants were never found. If Grantham and Victoria continued to thwart and harass her at every turn, she'd continue to do this—stay by her husband's side and wait on God.

She closed her eyes and prayed for strength and patience.

Because standing against the unknown was a lot easier said than done.

Chapter 15

"Achoo."

Priscilla pulled a tissue out of the rose-colored box Mama handed her.

Mama shook her head. "I knew it was too soon and too cold out yesterday for you to take that walk. I should've put my foot down and insisted you and Liz stay inside."

Priscilla stifled another sneeze and wiped at her nose. Mama didn't know that the culprit was likely the cold and damp grass she and Barry had laid on for almost an hour, and not the walk. Priscilla wasn't about to tell her. Barry felt bad enough about it already.

Mama handed her a cup of hot tea. "It's a new flavor, one of the vendors from the café introduced me to. It's supposed to have lots of natural healing properties in it for head colds. It tastes just like regular pomegranate tea to me, but we'll see if it does any good."

Priscilla sipped the tea and motioned for Mama to sit on the brown leather sofa across from her. Since the mornings were getting colder, Barry had gotten into the habit of stoking a roaring fire for her and Mama before he tended to the horses.

She'd never had the chance to start her *official* riding lessons. She hoped she'd be able to before it got too cold. She was glad Barry had allowed Francine to exercise Rich Brown until she could ride again.

Mama sat and tucked her legs beneath her. Priscilla continued to be amazed at how limber her mother was. Her seventy-seventh birthday was a few months away. She'd call Penelope later to see if she had any plans for Mama's birthday. If not, they needed to plan something soon.

"It was Grantham."

Priscilla furrowed her brow. "What was Grantham?"

"Grantham's the one behind the attack on you. I doubt he was the one behind the wheel, but he's definitely the one responsible. He's the one I saw in the vision. I told you I'd tell you when I had confirmation. Lydia and other prayer warriors have helped me seek God on the matter. I didn't tell them *who* I saw, but we're all in agreement that he's the one behind it."

Priscilla stared at Mama. She had on a pair of maroon velour joggers with a matching top that zipped near the collar. Her shiny silvery hair had been styled in a short sassy cut, and as always, contrasted beautifully against her smooth, and wrinkle-free dark skin.

She looked into her teacup, then around the room she'd redecorated with such care. Everything looked the same as it had a minute ago. Including Mama. So why did she feel like the world as she knew it had just fallen apart?

"Prissy? Did you hear what I said?"

She looked at Mama again. Did she just say something?

Mama stood, walked around the table between them, and sat next to Priscilla. She removed the teacup from Priscilla's hands and set it on the table. She placed her hands on Priscilla's cheeks and looked into her eyes. "Prissy, I need to know that you heard what I said."

"I don't … I don't know."

"You don't know what to say? Or you don't know what I said?"

Priscilla tried to lower her head, but Mama gave it a slight shake. "Pull yourself together."

Priscilla closed her eyes and desperately tried to gather her thoughts. She needed to say something quick before Mama slapped some sense into her. She'd been in this exact position with her mother too many times growing up. She knew she only had a couple of seconds.

"Mama, I … Grantham? Are you sure?"

"I am."

"But why?"

"Why does he want you dead?"

Priscilla nodded.

"My guess would be because you're standing in the way of them inheriting all of their daddy's money."

"I mean, I know that, but … wait. Victoria's trying to kill me, too?"

"I don't think so, but I'm not sure. That's why I didn't want you up there on that hill alone when she was here yesterday. Innocent or not, I still don't trust her."

"I don't either."

Mama placed her hands in her lap. "Either way, if Edith was alive, she'd be disappointed in those two. She was an amazing mom. But the older they got, the more stubborn they became. She was heartbroken when they'd returned from college, saying God was dead and Christianity was no longer for them. But she continued to pray for their souls. Which is why I wanted to take my time to make sure I was right about this. Out of respect for Edith."

After Daddy died, several members of his congregation had asked Mama to step in to fill his shoes. But Mama had said that she'd never felt the call to pastor, so it wasn't long before the small congregation went elsewhere.

Mama also wanted to find a thriving church community for her and her daughters. She'd tried several ones before she settled on Resurrection Church, which was where she'd met Edith. Barry, at the time, didn't attend church.

Her stomach clenched. What in the world was she going to tell Barry?

Mama continued. "Every morning Barry asks for a name and I say no. He asked again this morning, but I shooed him out the door. I wanted to talk to you first. Do you want me to tell him? Or are you going to do it?"

She wanted Mama to do it. And Priscilla didn't want to be within a hundred-mile radius of Barry when she did. She didn't want to see the look on her husband's face when Mama told him that his son had tried to kill his wife.

Priscilla swallowed. "I'll do it."

"Good. It'll sound better coming from you."

Would it? Yesterday, when she'd told him about Victoria, he'd walked away from her to go lay down in a clearing. It had taken a while, but afterwards, he was finally able to find peace. Now she had to shatter that peace once again.

How long would it be before he started to blame her?

No. Barry knew she'd had done nothing to provoke the attack on her. But would he begin to resent her?

Or regret marrying her?

They hadn't walked into this marriage blindly. They'd taken great care to take Grantham and Victoria's concerns into consideration. Barry never asked them to respect his decision to marry her, he just asked them to show her respect. They'd refused, but she and Barry had both hoped that over time, they'd at least try.

Instead, they'd secretly plotted to kill her.

At least Grantham had.

She had a hard time imagining he'd do something like that without getting his younger sister's input. He valued her opinion.

And usually did her bidding.

The few conversations she'd had with him had started

with the phrase *Victoria said.* Followed by *Victoria thought, Victoria wants me to,* or *Victoria doesn't think that's a good idea.*

They knew the difficulties that lay ahead regarding Grantham and Victoria, but they'd had no idea that behind their backs, plans were being made to take Priscilla out.

Literally.

When had things become so sinister?

A chill crawled up Priscilla's spine, and she shivered. Mama retrieved Priscilla's teacup from the side table. "I'll turn on the kettle and get you a fresh cup. I'll also add some honey, lemon, and whiskey."

Priscilla sneezed and grabbed another tissue from the holder. A hot toddy is just what she needed. "Can you also bring me a blanket?"

Mama pointed to the roaring fire, then furrowed her brows. "It's not cold in here."

The chill hadn't come from the temperature in the room. "Please, Mama?"

She agreed and walked toward the kitchen.

Priscilla pulled her phone from her pants pocket and dialed Barry.

He picked up after the first ring. "Morning, love."

"Morning." Priscilla sucked in a deep breath before continuing. "Are you nearby?"

She smacked her forehead. That was a dumb question, and it was sure to set off an alarm in Barry's brain. He hadn't left the property or worked at his office in downtown Habakkuk since the accident. Whatever business he'd had to conduct, he'd done from his home office.

After a pause he said, "Of course I am. You know I'm not going anywhere until the guy who ran you off the road is caught. What's going on, Silly?"

Yep. She'd blown it. Her plan had been to just ask him to come to the house so that they could have coffee together. Then she'd tell him what Mama had said after he was sitting down.

"Where are you?"

"In the barn, checking the horse's water buckets."

That was normally a part of Shields' job. She never got around to asking him how his conversation with the stable hand had gone. Or how long he'd agreed to let him off work.

"Silly?"

"I'm here. Do you mind coming back to the house? I want to talk to you about something."

He let out a ragged breath before answering. "Go ahead and tell me now. I can tell by your tone that it's not good news."

"You want to be sitting for this one, Barry. Trust me."

"I prefer to be standing when I hear bad news. Just say it. Don't sugarcoat it."

Priscilla bowed her head. *Lord, surround Barry with Your comfort and give us wisdom.*

"Silly, you there?"

"I am."

"What is it you wanted to tell me?"

"Mama told me who she saw in her vision." She paused and wiped at a tear that threatened to escape. "It was Grantham."

Barry cleared his throat, but he didn't respond.

"Obviously, he wasn't the one driving the car since he was in police custody at the time. But she believes that he's the one who orchestrated it."

Silence.

Priscilla stood. "Which barn are you in?"

More silence.

"Barry?"

"I'm in the … don't worry about it, Silly. I'll be okay."

She gritted her teeth. "Didn't we just have a conversation about this yesterday? You're not in this alone."

"Give me an hour, then I'll make my way back up to the house."

"What do you need an hour for?"

"To think and pray over some things. To call the Sheriff."

"The Sheriff? For what?"

"To ask him to look into Grantham as a possible suspect in the hit-and-run."

"You don't have to do that. I'm not going to press charges against your son."

"It may not be up to you. Or me."

"The police don't have to know about this at all, Barry. Let's just take a few days and talk it through. Together."

"Prissy, he has to tell them." Priscilla looked over her shoulder. Mama was standing so close that their noses almost touched. "Does Barry have a life insurance policy on you?"

Priscilla nodded. They had insurance policies on each other.

Mama placed a hand on her hip. "Then if you don't want your husband to be considered a suspect, you better let him tell the police what he knows. If he waits, they'll find that suspicious."

"Suspicious?"

Barry's voice came through the speaker. "Mabel's right."

She looked at her mother while answering Barry. "I'm not saying we don't tell them. I just don't want to rush into anything."

Mama moved to stand in front of her. "If you don't want your husband hung up on a conspiracy to commit murder charge, then let the man do what he needs to do."

Chapter 16

"Oh, Pris."

Liz dropped a large cardboard box between them and sat cross-legged next to Priscilla on the floor. "I had no idea things had gotten so bad between you and Grantham."

"Neither did I."

Yesterday, after her conversation with Barry, he'd called the Sheriff, who'd decided he needed more information. He'd interviewed her, Mama, and Barry. To the Sheriff's credit, he didn't snicker, smile, or laugh when Mama had told him about her vision. He did say that it wouldn't be enough to go on, but the incident between Priscilla and Grantham at the shopping center was. He'd radioed one of his deputies and told him to go check out the surveillance footage. Then his deputy forwarded the footage to the Sheriff. After reviewing the hate-filled tirade, he agreed to look further into Grantham and his finances.

Liz lifted the lid off the box. When Priscilla had called her, she'd been working at Penelope's medical office. Apparently, Penelope was way behind in sending out her patient's invoices, so she jumped at the chance when Liz had offered to help.

Penelope was so glad she'd been relieved of the time-consuming task that she didn't blink an eye when Priscilla asked if Liz could spend the rest of the afternoon stuffing invoices into envelopes at her place.

"I knew Grantham and Victoria were upset about me inheriting the property, but upset enough to kill me for it?"

Liz placed the lid next to her. "This property is worth a small fortune. People have done a lot worse for a lot less money."

"I know. But if I'd died in that accident, Barry still wouldn't have changed his mind about Grantham and Victoria inheriting the property. He didn't want them to have it."

"Did he ever say why?"

"Grantham had been approached a few years ago by another commercial developer who'd wanted to buy the property. They wanted to tear down everything and build condominiums. Apparently, they'd tried talking with Barry first, but he'd told them to get lost. After that, they paid Grantham to urge his father to sell."

"They paid him?"

Priscilla nodded.

"What a dirtbag. I can't believe Grantham would do something like that. Surely he knows how much his father loves this place."

"Oh, he knows. But Grantham's mind always seems to be on money."

"What happened when Barry refused?"

"The company moved on, but not before they demanded their money back from Grantham."

Liz's eyes widened. "Ouch. How much was that?"

"Quarter of a million."

"Seriously?"

"Yeah, but he couldn't pay it back. He'd already spent the money, so he asked his dad for it."

"Let me guess. Barry said, *dude you must be crazy*."

Priscilla laughed. "Pretty much."

"So, there's been tension between them for a while now?"

"Yep."

Liz pulled a handful of invoices from the box. "Now, all of this is starting to make sense. Grantham was already mad at his dad for not selling the property and then for not bailing him out of that stupid deal. Then you come along. When he realized your relationship with Barry was serious, both he and Victoria hired investigators to look into your background, hoping to find something that'll dissuade their dad from marrying you, but Barry already knew everything."

"Plan A didn't work, so they started shaking in their boots. A wife for their dad meant they'd have to share their inheritance. And when Barry updated his will to make you the sole heir of the property, they realized they had to come up with a Plan B, because now they wouldn't be able to sell it to the highest bidder."

"Perhaps. And maybe it wouldn't have happened that way if Grantham wasn't always so desperate for money. That's why Barry wasn't going to leave the property to him. Or Victoria. She'd never made any type of ridiculous proposal like Grantham did to her dad, but he didn't trust her to not sell the property either."

"And they didn't know that no matter what happened to you, they weren't going to inherit it?"

"Barry never told them. They weren't interested in keeping the property anyway, so he didn't think it'd be a big deal. It wasn't like he's not going to leave them anything. Over a third of his entire estate goes to them and their families."

Liz folded one of the invoices and slid it into an envelope. "Greed."

"What?"

"I guess a third wasn't enough. They wanted

everything."

Priscilla grabbed another stack of invoices from the box and folded them in silence next to Liz.

She didn't care that they wanted everything. If Barry changed his mind tomorrow and removed her completely from his will, it wouldn't bother her a bit. What bothered her is that she almost died for nothing.

Liz nudged her. "You okay?"

"Still trying to process it all, I guess."

"Any updates from the police?"

"Not since yesterday."

"Well, if I were you, I'd ask Barry to have a conversation with his kids. He needs to let them know that there's no way they'll ever get their hands on this property."

"Why?"

"Because as long as they think there's a chance, you're in danger."

Priscilla gasped. "You think they'd try to finish the job?"

"Yes. Murder-for-hire folks don't work for free. I bet Grantham paid the person who tried to run you off the road a handsome amount and promised him even more if he was successful. If Grantham thinks he still has a chance of inheriting this land, the guy may still be on his payroll. Biding his time until things cool down. Where's Grantham now, anyway?"

"Out on bail. He and his wife are staying with Victoria."

"I saw her the other day when I was here. She was visiting Barry?"

"Yeah. Then she stopped to say hi to me on her way out."

"That was nice. But I'd still be careful around her."

"Mama said the same thing. Victoria's always Victoria, you know, but I think she may have been trying to extend an olive branch the other day."

"How so?"

"She wanted to show me one of her favorite spots in the hills. Well, actually she said it was a favorite of the family, lots of childhood memories there. She knows how I love the views from Peace Hill and she wanted to show me the one from their favorite spot. It sounds amazing."

"Did she say where it was?"

"Not really, but she did say she and Grantham gave it the nickname of Bad Man's Slope when they were kids."

"Bad Man's Slope? Shields told me about that place. He and a few of the other workers liked to go up there and hangout when their shifts were over. He said the views are spectacular. But when Barry found out, he told them not to go up there anymore."

Priscilla stamped the envelopes. "Did he say why?"

"Barry said it was too dangerous and Shields agreed. The incline to get up there is steep and slippery, and you had to be really careful when you made it to the top because of all the cliffs.

Shields also said you didn't need to be near the edge to be in danger of falling. Something about how the weather had deteriorated a lot of the surroundings. The guys loved it up there, but they were always careful. None of them wanted to see if they'd survive a ninety-foot drop."

Liz flicked her gaze to Priscilla. "I know Victoria's been up there recently, because Shields said he ran into her one day while they were there. She knows how dangerous it is now, so why would she invite you to go up there?"

Priscilla locked eyes with Liz. She didn't need to answer the question because it was apparent they were thinking the same thing.

Had Victoria planned to push Priscilla over the edge?

Make it look like an accident?

Tell Barry and Mama that Priscilla had somehow slipped and fell?

No. That would've been too risky. So soon after Priscilla's hit-and-run would've looked awfully suspicious to the police.

But maybe not. Grantham hadn't been a suspect then. And neither had Victoria.

And she still wasn't.

But should she be?

Chapter 17

Priscilla wanted to call Barry.

She wanted him to know the concerns she and Liz had about Victoria.

But what did they really have besides speculation? Nothing.

And *nothing* wasn't worth adding to Barry's pain.

Besides, as far as they knew, Victoria had planned to do exactly what she'd said she'd wanted to do—show Priscilla an amazing view.

But if that was the case, why had Victoria gotten so angry when Priscilla refused to go?

She shook her head. She wasn't going to do this. She wasn't going to question anyone's motives unless she had a good reason to do so.

Well, a good reason backed by evidence.

Liz wrapped a rubber band around a thick stack of stuffed envelopes and tossed them back into the box. She looked at the stack of invoices beside her. "Just this pile to go, then I'm headed to the post office. Thanks for helping. I didn't think I'd get done with these until later this evening, close to the start of the game."

"What game?"

"Shields plays tonight. The Habakkuk Lions have a game against a team from St. Louis. Can't think of the name."

Priscilla giggled. "I'm surprised you actually remember the name of the team your boyfriend plays on. You never were into sports."

"Fiance." She handed Priscilla half of the stack next to her. "He's my fiancé, remember? Not my boyfriend. And I'm not into sports, just baseball."

"That's a sport."

"Well, I'm just into the team Shields plays for. It's exciting sitting in the seats and cheering him on. I like it a lot. Who knew going to a ballgame could be so much fun?"

"Oh, I don't know. Maybe about a million people."

"I've been to his games. All of them combined don't come close to a million people. At last week's game, there was maybe two to three hundred."

"I was talking about *professional* baseball. You know, the games that are played in the big stadiums?"

"I don't know about those, but I know my fiancé is a great player."

"How would you know? You don't even understand the game."

"I know a little. Shields has been trying to explain it to me."

"What position does he play?"

"Shortstop."

Priscilla lifted her brows. "Wow, I'm impressed you knew that."

Liz chuckled. "Yeah, I am too."

"If you're going to the games, I take it things are still going strong between the two of you?"

"It is." Liz tilted her head back and looked at the ceiling. "Watching him practice, going to the games, living and working with Penelope, it's been good for me." She lowered her gaze. "Helps keep my mind busy."

Priscilla caught her friend's eyes. "How have you been doing?"

"Well, I now have more good days than bad. Your sister thinks I'd benefit from joining a support group."

"What kind of support group?"

"I'm not sure of the name, but it's for adult survivors of childhood abuse. She said someone named Ruth holds a weekly meeting at the church you guys attend."

Priscilla nodded. "Ruth Greene, our pastor's wife. If she's running it, I think it'll be worth your while to go. I've heard great things."

"What if she finds out that I'm not a Christian?"

"Everyone's welcome to go to those support groups. Being a Christian is not a requirement."

Liz clicked her tongue. "I get it. I'll receive support, but not the full extent of it. If I want that, I'd have to accept Jesus. Am I right?"

"There's no bait and switch, Liz. You only accept Christ if you want to, but if you don't, no one's going to force you to. And both Christians and non-Christians receive the same type of support."

Liz ran a hand through her blonde waves. "I'm not sure I'll be able to do it."

"Do what?"

"Talk about everything that happened with a group of strangers."

"I think it might help to know that you're not alone."

"Penelope also thinks a lot of the decisions I've made in my life stem from what happened to me."

"What do you think?"

A couple of seconds passed by before she responded. "Despite everything my parents did to me, I don't ever remember hating them. As I matter of fact, I know I didn't. I loved them, and I desperately wanted them to love me back.

"I did everything I could to make them happy, to make them love me. But it was never enough. If I did everything they asked, I got in trouble. If I *didn't* do what they asked, I got in trouble. I cried a lot, but it wasn't from hunger pains or the beatings, it was because nothing I did pleased them."

She sucked in a deep breath and let it out in short, ragged bursts. "I was devastated when they went to prison. How could I make them happy if they weren't around? But Sharla told me to forget about them and everything that happened and focus on my future. I absorbed everything she taught me and that's what led to the decisions I made in my life, not my childhood."

"Who's Sharla?"

"That's who I was sent to live with when my parents were arrested. You know, the *family member*." She air quoted the last two words.

Liz had mentioned before how the news outlets had gotten it wrong about her going to live with a family member, but until now, she'd never said who it was.

"If she wasn't a family member, who was she?"

"Sharla and my mom grew up together. They were raised in the same foster home. She was the closest thing my mom had to a sister."

"What did she teach you?"

"How to please the people who really mattered."

"I don't understand."

"She taught me how to use what I had to get what I wanted. The side benefit for me was when someone I'd *pleased* asked for a return visit. I'd made them happy. They'd liked me. Wanted me around. They smiled when I entered the room. I didn't know how much I'd needed that until then. It was addictive, like a drug."

Acid churned in Priscilla's stomach. Liz had only been nine-years-old.

"And as much as I'd loved Henry, I soon realized that if I played my cards right, I'd never have to depend on a mouse to bring me food ever again."

Priscilla opened her mouth to say something, then closed it. Her stomach needed to settle before she attempted to speak. She didn't want to vomit on the paperwork surrounding them.

Liz leaned against the couch behind them and stared into her lap.

Priscilla needed a bucket or at least a trash can to empty her stomach into. The smart thing would be to excuse herself and go to the bathroom, but she wasn't going to do that. Liz was finally opening up about what had happened to her and no matter how disgusted Priscilla was, she wasn't going to let an upset stomach pull her away. Liz needed her comfort. Not her puke.

Priscilla cleared her throat. "What, um… what happened to Sharla? I've known you for a long time, and I've never heard you mention her before."

"She was murdered. I found her strangled one night in her bedroom."

Priscilla gasped. "Liz, I'm so sorry."

She shrugged. "It was bound to happen sooner or later. She played loose and free with her love. Was emotionally entangled with several of her clients."

"Still, after everything you'd already been through—"

"It all worked out. Sharla had a beautiful home in Kansas. I was old enough to be on my own by then, but I continued staying there for a while and lived the way she'd taught me."

"Eventually, I made my way back here." She scratched her cheek. "My parents were arrested when I was nine. I was in my early twenties when Sharla was killed. I spent more time with her than I did with my parents. So, to answer your question, I don't think what my parents did to me led to the poor decisions I've made or the lifestyle I chose. Sharla had more of an influence on me than they did, but in the end, I was the one who'd decided how I wanted to live."

"You were still a child when you were sent to live with Sharla."

Liz furrowed her brows. "I was, wasn't I?" She shook her head. "Hard for me to picture myself as a child back then."

Priscilla wasn't surprised. "Listen, regardless of when or where it all started, I still think the church support group would be good for you. You could talk it over with Ruth one on one. Maybe there's some inner healing that needs to take place."

"That sounds similar to something Penelope said. But that's my point. There's nothing to heal. I'm not mad at my parents or Sharla. Were they right in what they did to me or the situations they put me in? No. But I don't resent them, and I'm not bitter. Neither of my parents knew how to take care of a child because no one had ever properly taken care of them, and Sharla showed me how to survive. They all did the best they could with the know how they had."

Priscilla tightened her lips. There were several things she wanted to say about the way Liz's parents treated her and how Sharla took advantage of the situation, but now was not the time.

"You don't have to be mad at someone for inner healing to take place." Priscilla leaned toward her. "Didn't you say that you started feeling down when you stopped being an escort?"

Liz nodded.

"Then maybe it's more about you not knowing who you are anymore. You've proudly engaged in that lifestyle for over forty years. You'd even earned a nickname from it. Many people around here still refer to you as Diamond Liz."

"And I won't apologize for my love of diamonds. But that wasn't why I continued living that way. I liked the responses I got."

"I know, and that's what I mean. You're no longer willing to do that for any type of response. And though you're older now than when you started, you're still as stunning as ever, and can go back to it any time you choose. But I think you've come to the place where you want more out of your life. A lot more."

"Like what?"

"I don't know, but I think that's what you're struggling with."

"I want what I had, but I'm no longer comfortable doing what I had to do to get it. Is that the point you're trying to make?"

"Essentially, but I'm not exactly doing a good job at it, which is why I'm *glad* you have Penelope, and also why I'm encouraging you to talk with Ruth, or join the group. What harm could come of it?"

"I could walk away feeling more depressed than I am now."

"That's not going to happen."

"How do you know?"

How did she know? Truth was, she didn't. She'd never been a part of a support group of any kind.

"I don't know much about the group, but I know Ruth Greene well enough to know the last thing you'd feel when you walk away from her is depressed."

Liz gathered the envelopes around them and put them all in the box. "There's a meeting this Saturday morning. I'll let you know how it goes. But if I hate it, I swear I'm not going back."

"And I won't ask you to."

Liz placed the lid back on the box and smiled. "Thanks for listening."

"Anytime. I wish I could go to the post office with you, but—"

"Oh, don't worry about it. Barry and your mom are right in not wanting you to leave the estate. There's security here and until everything is cleared with Grantham, it's best that you stay close. Besides," She wiggled her shoulders back and forth and gave a toothy grin. "I have a game to go to tonight."

"I hope the Lions win. But tell Shields that even if the team loses, he's still a winner."

"He is?"

"He has you, doesn't he?"

Liz's eyes filled with tears. "Thank you for that, Pris."

Priscilla gave her a hug. "I love you so much. Don't ever forget that."

Liz nodded against her shoulder.

"I had my doubts about you and Shields' relationship and how fast it's been moving, but anyone with eyes can see how much he loves you. He adores you, Liz."

She sobbed. Priscilla pulled a tissue from her sweater pocket and handed it to her.

Liz took a step back and wiped her eyes before picking up the box. Priscilla walked her to the front door.

As she pulled out of the driveway, Priscilla prayed, *Lord, please show Liz that the only One worth pleasing is You.*

Chapter 18

"How dare you?"

Priscilla flicked the bedroom television off with the remote and looked toward the doorway. It was Grantham's wife.

Priscilla slid her socked feet off the cushioned bench she'd had them on. "Margaret. What are you doing here?"

"Did you tell the police that my husband tried to kill you?"

Priscilla stood and let the remote drop into the chair. "No, I did not."

"Then why did they confiscate all of our computers and phones?"

She stepped towards Margaret. She wished she'd had on her heeled slippers. Without them, she and Margaret were about the same height. Margaret's rigid posture, long neck, and upturned nose had a way of making Priscilla feel looked down upon. And Margaret's smug tone didn't help.

"Because he's a suspect in a hit-and-run."

Margaret used the back of her hand to toss a long, dark braid across her back. "Grantham was in jail at the time. He was nowhere near your accident."

"It wasn't an accident. Someone tried to kill me."

"Well, it wasn't him, so why is he a suspect?"

Priscilla stared into Margaret's steely-gray eyes. "Because he hates me. *I* never told the police that it was him, but because of his behavior towards me—a lot of it documented, such as the store footage—*they* were the ones who'd decided he was worth looking into."

"And who pointed the police in his direction?"

Mama walked up with her arms behind her back and stood next to Margaret. "I did."

Margaret whipped toward Mama. "You? Why?"

"I've got my reasons. And I'll gladly share them with you when you leave Prissy's room and come downstairs."

"Downstairs? What for? I'm not going anywhere until I give *Prissy*," she spat out the last word. "A piece of my mind."

"Right now you're blocking the door, and I can't have that. Step away so Prissy can get out."

Margaret huffed and leaned against the doorjamb, her back toward Mama. "Go away, old woman."

Priscilla saw a flash of metal before Margaret let out a quick scream. Priscilla's heart raced. *No, Lord, please, no. Please don't tell me Mama just put her Colt .45 into Margaret's back.*

Mama stood on her toes to get closer to Margaret's ear. "I'm not playin' with you, lil girl. I said, get out of my daughter's way."

Margaret pushed off the door frame and ran down the hallway. "Crazy! You're crazy!" When she started down the stairs, Priscilla grabbed the gun from Mama. "What are you doing? You can't just jam guns into people's backs like that, Mama."

"I'm licensed."

"That's not the point. Why did you even bring it up here with you?" Mama normally kept her weapon in her purse.

"Her husband hired someone to kill you, Prissy. For all I know, she came up here to finish the job."

Priscilla laid the gun on her dresser. Mama was right. Because Margaret was family, she doubted the guards had checked her for weapons. The only one at this point that was banned from entering the property was Grantham. And with the police looking at him as a suspect, no way would he try to visit. But obviously, that didn't stop his wife.

What was the real reason Margaret stopped by? Was it really just to give Priscilla a piece of her mind? Or was she planning something more?

Priscilla shook her head to erase that last thought. She had to be careful. Now was not the time to become paranoid.

Mama rubbed Priscilla's back. "You okay?"

Priscilla nodded as her cell phone dinged. Barry sent a text wanting to know why Margaret had run out of the house crying.

She texted him back, *Mama pulled a gun on her.*

Priscilla's phone rang.

She tapped it on and whispered to Mama, "It's Barry. I'll be downstairs in a few minutes."

"Tell him everything's fine here." She sang out as she walked down the hall.

Priscilla placed the phone next to her ear. "Hey."

"What in the world?"

She could hear the frustration in his voice and her heart hurt. She needed to explain what had happened without making it worse. "I'm in the bedroom watching a movie. Margaret came in and demanded to know why I told the police to look into Grantham. I guess Mama heard her, so she asked Margaret to get away from my door. Margaret said no, then Mama pulled out her .45."

Barry chuckled. At least she hoped it was a chuckle. And not one of those psychotic breaks that led to the type of laugh that preceded a mental breakdown.

"You okay, Barry?"

He chuckled again. "I'm okay. I was just imagining the look on Margaret's face when Mabel pulled out her .45."

Priscilla laughed with him. "Actually, it was quite funny, especially the way she tucked tail and ran down the hall. Before that she was all bravado and sass. Even called Mama an old woman."

He guffawed. "What? And she left without a bullet in her backside?"

"Barely."

"I was walking to the front of the house and saw her running down the front steps. I asked if she was okay and that's when I noticed she was crying. She ignored me and got into her car. I just figured the two of you had gotten into an argument."

"Nope. I'm innocent. That was all Mabel Martin."

"Sorry I missed it."

"Where are you now?"

"Headed to my office for a couple of virtual meetings. Why don't you come downstairs and join me?"

Priscilla looked at the ratty jeans and mustard-stained sweatshirt she wore. Everything she had on was made for comfort. Did she really want to change into a blouse and slacks? No, she didn't.

"Anything for you, love. Give me a minute to change into something more professional."

"Professional?"

"Yeah. I was thinking one of my long-sleeve blouses with—"

"I was thinking that silky, little nightgown I bought for your birthday."

"Barry!"

"What? You're not going to be on camera."

"I'm not? Then what will I be doing?"

"Offering me a distraction. It's been a long day. Not sure I'll be able to keep my eyes open for the meeting. You sitting on the other side of my desk will help with that."

Priscilla shook her head. If she sat across from him in the tiny little thing he was suggesting, he'd be more than distracted. No. She'd caused enough trouble the past couple of weeks with his family. She didn't want to start now with his work. He needed to focus.

"How about I save the gown for later and bring you down a hot cup of coffee?"

"Grrr."

"I know, but then you'll be wide awake for your meeting."

"If you say so."

"Aww, cheer up. I'll have something nice waiting for you when you're done."

"Oh, really? I'm distracted now just thinking about it."

"You oughtta be."

Several chirps and voices sounded in the background. He cleared his throat. "Gotta go. Time for me to start the meeting."

"See you soon." She tapped the phone off and smiled. She'd succeeded. She'd lightened her husband's mood. She'd helped take him from frustrated to expectant.

She glared at the gun on the dresser.

Now … to deal with Mama.

Chapter 19

Mama knocked on the bedroom door. "Time to come up for air, you two. It's almost noon. You've gotta be starving by now."

Priscilla giggled and Barry chuckled.

Priscilla could only imagine what Mama thought they'd been up to and, apparently, Barry had imagined the same thing.

Truth was, they'd been up and dressed for hours. It was rainy, cold, cloudy, and gloomy out, so they'd stayed in. Priscilla'd rifled through their bedroom closet and found the one-thousand-piece puzzle of the Holy Land their friends Ethan and Mary had given them last Christmas. They'd been meaning to work on it for months, but had never found the time.

Mama knocked again.

Priscilla slid a piece of the Jordan River into place. "I told you having Mama stay in the main house with us was a bad idea. She's too nosey. And she never wants to stop feeding us."

Barry chuckled. "Why do you think I've spent so much

time working with the stable hands? I'm trying to work off the ten pounds I've gained since Mabel moved in."

"Oh, I'm not even going to *dare* step on a scale. Last time I told Mama she's the reason I've gained weight, she rolled her eyes and handed me one of her homemade croissants. I'm telling you, I can't keep living like this." She looked down at her waist. Was that a pudge?

Mama tried the door handle. Thankfully, they'd locked it earlier.

"She also has major issues with boundaries." Barry turned toward the door. "We're awake Mabel. We'll be down in a few."

He turned to Priscilla. "But there's no way I could've asked my mother-in-law to stay in the guest house. Especially after your accident. She wouldn't have agreed, anyway. She was determined to stay close to you."

"I know, and cooking for people is like her love language or whatnot, but still, she can be a bit much. Frankly, I'm surprised she even wants to look at me this morning."

"Your conversation last night didn't go well?"

"I just needed her to see how the situation with Margaret could've easily backfired. What if Margaret had gone to the police and said Mama had threatened her with a gun? Or if she'd tried to take the gun from Mama?" Priscilla closed her eyes to squeeze out that thought. Mama wasn't a novice when it came to guns. She visited the gun range regularly and had won a couple of awards for skeet shooting as well. Margaret was younger, but she doubted she was stronger than Mama, who'd been active in senior aerobics classes for years. And Mama had been overly protective of Priscilla ever since they'd come home from the hospital. If Mama had shot Margaret, that would've made Barry's relationship with Grantham a million times worse than it was already. And right now, it was pretty bad.

Barry placed another piece of the puzzle in place.

"Margaret's all bark and no bite. And the only reason she's concerned about the police checking into Grantham is because of how it'll affect her. She doesn't love Grantham. Never has. She only married him for his money, and that's the only reason she's stayed so long."

Priscilla looked across the table at Barry. "Say what?"

"It's true. He loves her, though. A lot. They met in college. Her parents are nice people, but her dad has struggled with addiction for a long time and has lost several jobs because of it. She graduated with a lot of debt. She told Grantham if he paid off her student loans, she'd agree to marry him. So he did."

"Seriously?"

Barry nodded. "Of course, Grantham didn't have a job at the time so technically *I* was the one who paid that debt."

Priscilla narrowed her eyes. "Let me guess. He didn't tell you he was going to do that, did he?"

"Nope. But his first job out of college was at King Global, so I made sure his salary reflected that debt. Margaret wasn't happy about it. When the money was repaid, she demanded I double his salary."

"Please tell me you didn't do that."

He gave her a look that left no doubt that the question had offended him. "I did not, but that hasn't stopped her from being a pain in my side. She constantly put pressure on Grantham to ask for more money."

Priscilla moved several parts of Galilee around the puzzle table. The few interactions she'd had with Grantham and Margaret as a couple weren't the best, and they always centered on money, but she'd thought they were at least happily married. Well, not happily. She'd witnessed several times where Grantham would reach for Margaret's hand, and she'd reluctantly give it to him. She didn't smile, and she definitely didn't seem to enjoy it. Tolerated it was more like it. Now at least she knew why.

"But you think he loves her, right?"

"I know he does. When things were good between the two of us, he'd confide in me about their relationship. He mentioned several times how he wished she longed for his love as much as he did for hers."

How sad. Priscilla tried to wrap her mind around being in a loveless marriage. How lonely that had to be.

Grantham was the one who'd always started arguments with them about money, so she'd assumed he was the one who was money hungry. But now she wondered if it had been Margaret all along. Maybe Grantham went along with it to get Margaret to love him.

Barry rubbed the back of his neck. "He's completely under her thumb. Or at least he was. Now that he's no longer working at King Global, and facing possible time in prison for the assault on the officer, she's been calling and asking if she can work in Grantham's position while their attorney's work on his case."

"Is she insane? And she had the audacity to call Mama crazy."

"I know, and I told her there was no way that was going to happen, but she seems desperate for money. And for the life of me, I can't figure out why. Grantham was paid very well, and they lived in one of my properties rent free. The company leased the cars they drove. The grandkids go to those ridiculously expensive boarding schools, but even then there's no way they should be struggling financially. Even with Grantham out of work. I know he has plenty of savings, along with several other investments."

Priscilla hiked her brow. "How do you know that?"

"He uses my accountant. I asked him about Grantham's investments and he showed me." He scratched at his chin. "Hmmph."

"What is it?"

"Margaret's name wasn't on any of his investments. Not even the savings account. The kids were named, but not Margaret."

Priscilla sat back in her chair. "Why wouldn't he have his wife's name on those accounts?"

Barry stared at the table.

A minute later, he flicked his gaze to Priscilla. "I don't think she knows about them."

"Why would he keep her in the dark about that?"

"He loves her, but I never got the feeling that he trusted her."

"Oh, Barry." Priscilla couldn't believe she was actually feeling sorry for Grantham. He'd never said one kind word to her—ever. His hatred of her was real. It was in his eyes. But she remembered a phrase her friend Eve had used when she'd asked for advice on how to handle Grantham. She'd said something along the lines of *hurting people hurt people.*

Eve was big on forgiveness and any wisdom she shared generally traveled down that road. She'd wanted Priscilla to try to understand Grantham and where his pain was coming from.

That had been hard to do since he'd refused to have a decent conversation with her. But was he in pain? Was he, like his sister Victoria, still struggling with the loss of their mother? Did they think Priscilla was trying to take their mother's place? She'd never do that. Though she made the mistake once of referring to Grantham and Victoria as her son and daughter. It was a year ago, on a day that Lola was visiting. Lola had understood Priscilla had meant stepson and stepdaughter, but Victoria had been there and had overheard. She'd gone ballistic and made it very clear that Priscilla wasn't her mother, stepmother, or any other type of mother except the foul one.

Then she'd stormed out of the house.

Grantham stopped by several minutes later, and echoed his sister's sentiments.

Priscilla never again made that mistake. Not even with Barry. She was afraid if she'd used those terms in casual everyday conversations with her husband, she'd let it slip again when they were around. The last thing she wanted was a repeat performance.

She'd hoped to be able to refer to them as *our* son and *our* daughter, not *his* son or *his* daughter. She was married to their dad, and she'd wanted them to know that she was open to them being an important part of her life as well.

But after that incident, she'd let it drop.

It never crossed her mind that after so many years, they'd still have such a strong reaction to their father remarrying.

Was it that? Or something else?

Could Grantham be lashing out at her, because his father had something *he* didn't? A marriage full of love, respect, and trust? A wife who adored him?

Was he putting all of his anger on her, because he couldn't do it with Margaret?

Or was all of it—with Victoria, Grantham, and Margaret—fueled by the ravenous and insatiable pull of greed?

So many questions.

So few answers.

Chapter 20

Barry's phone was on the table.

It had vibrated, slid into the streets of Jerusalem, and collided with the Mount of Olives before Priscilla had the chance to pick it up.

She handed it to Barry. "Looks like we missed whoever was calling."

He was about to toss it on the bed when it rang again. He answered and put it on speaker.

"Boss, it's me, Shields."

Barry chuckled. "I have caller I.D., Shields."

"Right. Wanted you to know a couple of the hands spotted a guy creeping around in the woods. When they asked why he was there, he ran off. They caught him, though. Sheriff's sending someone out now."

Priscilla's eyes widened.

Barry stood. "On my way."

He shoved the phone in his back pocket. "Stay inside the house. I'll be right back."

"Barry." She stood and placed a hand on his arm. "Don't go yet. Let's wait until the police arrive."

He gently pulled his arm away. "I'll be back soon."

"We don't know if he's the only one. There could be more of them in the woods."

He walked to the bedroom door.

She plopped down in her chair. Maybe if she faked a tantrum, it would delay him long enough for the police to arrive. She didn't know who the guy was or what he wanted, but it couldn't have been anything good since he was trespassing. There were many signs and wire-fencing throughout the wooded areas marked private property. No way he could've missed them.

Barry looked over his shoulder at her. He opened his mouth, closed it, then opened the bedroom door.

Priscilla followed him down the stairs and into the kitchen. He grabbed his black Stetson from the peg rail and exited through the back door.

Mama sat at the table eating a taco salad and reading through one of Chef Rigalta's recipe books. "Chef's a good guy. He's doing a nice job holding down the fort at the café for me. But I'll never understand his disdain for salt. None of the recipes in his cookbook call for it. Eve has had to remind him more than once that when a customer requests one of my dishes, he can't omit the salt."

"He thinks salt is unhealthy." Priscilla pulled out a chair and sat. "Mama, one of the stable hands just called. They found a man prowling around in the woods."

Mama looked up from the book. "Salt comes from the earth. God created the earth. Salt is good."

"Mama, did you hear me?"

"I heard you. Is that why Barry left out of here in such an all-fire hurry?"

"The guys are holding the man until the police arrive. I think Barry wants to talk to him before they get here."

"Who called the police?"

Priscilla shrugged. "I don't know. One of the stablemen maybe?"

"Shields, probably."

"He's Barry's top guy, so that would make sense. He's also the one who called to let Barry know what happened."

"I like Shields." Mama flipped a page in the book, then went back to reading.

Priscilla studied Mama. She didn't seem a bit concerned about the strange man found in the woods.

"Mama, did you know they'd find a man in the woods?"

She looked up from the book. "How in the world would I know something like that?"

Priscilla clicked her tongue. "I don't know, Mama. Maybe because you've been known to know about things before they happen?"

Mama closed the book. "I knew nothing about it."

"And you're not concerned?"

"About what?"

"A strange man on the property."

"Why would I be? You said Shields and the guys handled it. And that the police are on their way."

Priscilla looked out the large glass window next to the breakfast table. With the blinds raised, it normally let in tons of sunshine in the afternoon hours. Today, the light coming into the kitchen area was dim. She was surprised Mama could even read by it.

She'd thought Mama'd be more upset about the news. More… reactionary. She remembered the time when she and Penelope were teens and a strange man tried to force his way through their front door in the middle of the night. Mama grabbed Daddy's old shotgun and blew a hole through the door.

She didn't ask the man what he'd wanted or who he was.

She'd just pulled the trigger.

The police had found duct tape, rope, and a large knife on the man. He'd survived Mama's shotgun blast, but he didn't survive prison. He was a known rapist.

Mama had always been fiercely protective of her and Penelope, and when Daddy died, even more so.

And now she had no reaction?

Mama cleared her throat. "As long as you're here in the house with me, Prissy, you'll be all right."

"I know, Mama. And it's not that. I guess I'm just not that used to you being so calm in a situation like this."

"I have my moments."

Priscilla laughed. "Apparently, you do."

"Besides, I don't feel a call to action in my spirit. When I do, I react. When I don't…" She picked up a tortilla chip loaded with beef, sour cream, cheese, jalapenos and salsa, and popped it into her mouth. When she was done, she wiped her mouth with a napkin and added, "I eat taco salad."

Priscilla took a plain tortilla chip from a basket in the center of the table and broke it in half before taking a bite of it. She loved these things, always had. The crispy saltiness had a way of satisfying her carb cravings like nothing else. She'd only have one. She had no impulse control when it came to the flavorful little chips.

"What are you wearing to the wedding?"

Priscilla stopped nibbling and looked at Mama. "What wedding?"

"Shields and Liz's wedding."

Priscilla hiked a brow. "You know about Shields and Liz?"

"Of course, I do."

"How?"

"I feed those guys three meals a day, Prissy. I know what's going on in their lives."

"You do what? Are you talking about the stable hands?"

"Yeah."

"You don't have to do that, Mama. They *work* here, they don't *live* here. They have homes they go to at the end of the day and wives and families. Why are you feeding them?"

"Because they like my cooking. And also because I've

seen some of the lunches those wives send with their husbands. Those men work hard. How are they supposed to survive on ham sandwiches and chips? One of the wives at least tries to send a hot meal for her husband. I tried her stew, though. It tasted like mud. No wonder he'd pour it on the ground and go out for fast food."

Priscilla didn't know if she wanted to laugh or be upset. It wasn't like the men were taking advantage of her mother. They hadn't asked her to cook for them. She'd taken it upon herself. It would've been nice if Mama'd told her about it, and if Mama was making them three meals a day, obviously Barry knew about it. He probably thought she knew about it, too.

What are you wearing to the wedding?

Wait a minute. Shields was talking to Mama about his relationship with Liz?

Why Mama and not her?

More importantly, what was Mama saying to Shields about Diamond Liz?

"Mama, do you and Shields talk a lot about Liz when you go over to the stables?"

Mama closed one of her eyes, as though she was thinking deeply on the subject. "Not really. We talk about a whole lot of other things. But he is getting married soon, so her name does come up."

Priscilla licked salty crumbs from her lips. Liz and Lola were not only her best friends, they were also like sisters. Mama loved them dearly and treated them like her daughters.

And Mama knew everything about them. From their childhood traumas to the type of lifestyles they'd lived because of those traumas.

"Well, just be careful when you're talking to Shields about Liz. He doesn't know about her past or how she made a living."

Mama furrowed her brows. "What do you mean? Yes,

he does."

"No, he doesn't. I talk to Liz all the time. She hasn't told him yet."

"When was the last time you talked to her?"

"She was just over here the other day."

"And she said nothing about telling Shields about her past?"

"Well, we've talked a lot about the topic, but no, she hasn't told him yet."

Mama looked down at the table, then out the window.

Priscilla's heart raced. Had Mama said something to Shields?

"He knows, Prissy."

"What do you mean?"

"He knows about her childhood and what her parents did to her. He knows she was an escort."

"Oh, Mama. What did you say to him?"

Mama turned to her. "I didn't have to say anything. When we've talked about Liz, it was as if he already knew about all of that."

Priscilla chewed her lip. Habakkuk was a small town. It was possible that he'd found out from someone else.

But why hadn't he said anything to Liz?

"Liz hasn't told him yet because she was afraid of how he'd react. She's fallen in love with him. She doesn't want to lose him."

"Shields isn't like that. He's a stand-up guy."

"I know, but still, that's a lot for someone to deal with. Liz and I have both known women who've lost out on love because they were former escorts. Men who'd loved them deeply, but who'd walked away because of the emotional and mental toll of it all."

"Liz was going to tell Shields, but their relationship brought up a lot of sad memories for her. She wanted to deal with those first, then tell him. Penelope's helping her with that, and she plans on attending a group meeting with Ruth

Greene at church tomorrow morning. Last I heard, she and Shields were taking it slow. I knew they were engaged, but she hasn't said anything to me about a wedding."

Mama pushed her salad to the side. "Does Liz know about Shields' past? About what happened to Ashley and his time in prison?"

Mama knew about that, too?

"I don't think she does, no. I haven't told her about it. I figured Shields would in time."

Mama gave a slow nod and looked out the window. "The police are here."

Priscilla followed her gaze. Three police cars drove by the window towards the stables. No sirens. Perhaps the guy *had* somehow stumbled onto their property. Their property line ended at a paved road that led into the forest. It was unlikely, but could've happened. Especially, if he'd lost something or was looking for someone. Maybe he'd had a dog that had run off? Could that be why he ignored the no trespassing warnings? Because not only were there signs, there were also trees and posts that had been marked with purple paint. Most Missouri residents were familiar with the Purple Paint statute and heeded the warnings.

Especially if they didn't want to get shot.

Priscilla's phone dinged.

She pulled it out. It was a text from Barry with an attached photo of the man found in the woods. He was young, perhaps in his late twenties, with a muscular build, brown eyes, and dark hair tied into a ponytail at the nape of his neck with a brown leather strap. He wore a white shirt under a black jean jacket.

Barry wanted to know if she'd ever seen him before. She replied she hadn't.

"Was that Barry?"

Priscilla turned her phone toward Mama. "He wanted to know if I'd ever seen this guy before."

Mama took the phone from Priscilla. "I know him. He

comes into the café a lot. The last couple times he's been there, he was with Margaret."

Priscilla's mouth fell open. Surely Mama didn't mean *Grantham's* wife Margaret.

"It looked like they had a little something-something going on. Eve and I have both seen them holding hands and looking into each other's eyes, all lover-like."

Priscilla swallowed. Was Margaret cheating on Grantham? With this guy? He was definitely handsome, but he was also young enough to be her son. "Mama, you're talking about Grantham's wife, right?"

Mama pinched her lips together before answering. "Of course I am. What other Margaret would I be talking about?"

"Just wanted to make sure." Priscilla took her phone back. "Does Margaret know you work at the café?"

"I doubt it. The only time I interact with the customers is when they have a question about the food or ask to compliment me personally. But I can easily see them when I glance out the galley windows. "

"Would you happen to know his name?"

Mama shook her head.

Priscilla called Barry. When he answered, she said, "Mama knows him. She's seen him at the café with Margaret."

"Really?"

"Yeah, and she also said that they looked like they were more than friends."

When Barry didn't respond, she asked, "Did he say what he was doing in our woods?"

"No. He hasn't said anything other than he wants a lawyer. He also doesn't have any ID on him. The police are taking him down to the station. They're going to see if they get a hit on his prints."

"He didn't have any weapons on him, did he?"

"Nothing was on him except a car key, so more than likely there's a car somewhere along the property line. The guys haven't found it yet and neither have the police. I'll let them know about the Margaret connection."

"Barry, I think you should call Grantham."

"I will, when I have more information."

"If Margaret or Grantham have ties to this guy, I think it'd be better if you heard it straight from Grantham's mouth. We should go to the station together."

Priscilla could almost hear his wheels turning. After a few seconds, he said, "No. I'll go. We still don't know exactly what's going on and you'll be safer here. I'll ask one of the officers to stay and watch the front of the house. The hands'll take care of the back. I'm sending Shields up to the house to stay with you and Mabel. I'll be back in an hour."

"Okay, love. Keep me updated."

"Will do." The call ended and Priscilla said, "Hopefully, this guy will be able to fill in some of the blanks."

Mama nodded and placed her lunch dishes in the sink.

Priscilla watched as two of the three police cars whizzed past again, this time toward the Habakkuk Hills main entrance.

LORD, thank You that this young man was caught, and that Mama remembered him from the café. I want to give him the benefit of the doubt, but can't think of any good reason why he would have been on our property. But I can think of a lot of bad ones.

Priscilla stared out the window. Had he been sent here to hurt her? Was he the driver of the car that ran her off the road? Was he working with Margaret? Grantham? Had they hired him to kill her?

Or was it somebody else entirely?

She was tired of being in the dark. She wanted answers. These people were playing with her life. Or at least someone was.

She looked at her phone. She had Margaret's number. She could call her.

She should call her.

Priscilla navigated to her contacts and pressed on the one labeled Margaret.

What should she say? She couldn't accuse the woman of something she had no evidence of. Maybe she should just hang up and continue to let the authorities handle it.

But there was no harm in asking her a question, right?

"What do you want?"

Priscilla yanked the phone from her ear and looked at it. Was this the way Margaret greeted everyone? Or just her?

Either way, she didn't have to take it.

Priscilla ended the call, then forwarded the photo of the guy to Margaret. In a separate text, she typed out, *Your boyfriend was found sneaking around our property. Now he's on his way to the police station.*

She hit send.

Her phone rang.

She lifted her phone and spoke directly into the mic. "What do you want?" If this was the type of conversation Margaret wanted to have, so be it.

Hissing, followed by a stream of foul language, flowed through the phone line. Margaret's voice came through loud and clear.

"You hear me?" Margaret's high-pitched tone screeched through Priscilla's ear piece. She imagined the amount of spittle that would've been coming her way if they'd had this conversation in person. Thank goodness she'd only called.

"You're going down, you gold-digging harlot." Margaret screamed in her ear. "Understand me? You're going down!"

Chapter 21

Someone knocked on the back door. Priscilla ended the call and opened it.

It was Shields, and he carried one of Barry's rifles.

She blew out a breath. "Hey."

"Hey." He stuck his head into the kitchen and looked around. "Everything, okay? You look upset."

"I'm fine, just trying to process a conversation I just had." Well, it wasn't really a conversation. She'd said one sentence. Margaret, on the other hand, had indulged in an entire rage-filled monologue. She was still ranting and raving when Priscilla'd ended the call.

"Were you talking to Barry? Did they find out who the guy was?"

"I haven't heard from him yet, but I'm glad that you're here. Do you mind if we sit on the back porch and talk a minute?"

"Sure."

Priscilla looked over her shoulder at Mama, who'd already started prepping for dinner. "I'm going outside with Shields."

"I heard you." Mama wiped her hands on a towel. "I'm standing right here."

She was also standing right there when Margaret had spewed her venom.

She'd listened, but hadn't said a word.

Highly unusual. She'd dissect that later with Mama. Right now, she needed to talk to Shields.

Priscilla grabbed her cardigan and scarf off the wooden peg and stepped onto the back porch. Shields sat on the stone wall surrounding the porch, and she sat in one of the vintage rockers next to it.

She wrapped the scarf around her. "Do you mind if I ask a few questions about your relationship with Liz?"

"I don't mind. What would you like to know?"

The aroma of sautéeing vegetables wafted their way. She checked to see if she'd completely shut the kitchen door behind her. She had. Apparently, the mouth-watering smells of butter, garlic, peppers, and onions had no boundaries.

She sniffed the air again and noticed that Shields had done the same. He was also smiling.

"I take it you like Mama's cooking?"

He nodded. "One of the downsides of being a bachelor and not living close to family is that home-cooked meals are rare."

"Your family's not in Missouri?"

His eyes narrowed. "No. My parents and younger sister live in Cheyenne."

"Wyoming?"

He gave a slow nod.

"That's a nice little distance away."

"We see each other often. Mostly holidays and birthdays, special occasions."

Priscilla gently rocked the chair back and forth. "Do they know about Liz?"

His brows lifted. "Um … Yeah. They're all looking forward to our trip there next summer."

"To Wyoming?" She'd asked casually enough, but wondered how successful she'd been at masking the surprise in her voice, and definitely her face. Liz hadn't said anything about traveling to see Shields' family.

His brows went from lifted to furrowed. "Yeah, Wyoming." He placed his thumb on his chin and leaned forward, his elbow resting on his thigh. "You're still coming, aren't you? I know how much Liz has been looking forward to you helping my mom and sister pick out a venue."

A venue? She pressed her lips together in an effort to stop asking further questions. The first one being, did he mean *a wedding venue?* Which would lead to another question she needed answered. Such as, *are the two of you getting married next summer in Wyoming?*

She didn't want to ask those questions because the look on his face told her he'd already thought she'd known the answers.

No wonder he'd been looking at her so strange.

But she hadn't known *any* of it. Especially the part about traveling to Wyoming.

She'd go to Mars and back if that's where Liz wanted to have her wedding. She didn't care where Liz got married. She cared that her best friend hadn't shared any of this with her.

Shields placed the rifle on the wall next to him. "Mrs. King, are you all right?"

She stopped the rocker and looked at Shields. She was not all right, but it wasn't his fault, it was his fiance's.

But what in the world was she to say to him now?

She didn't want him to know that Liz hadn't shared some of the most important details of her upcoming wedding with her. Heck, if it hadn't been for Mama, she wouldn't have known there was going to be an upcoming wedding. She'd known they were getting married, but the when and where had been a question mark.

At least to her.

"I'm okay. Today's just turning out a lot different from I'd expected."

He straightened and gave a slight nod. "I've had those types of days. I've learned to roll with them. They have a way of working themselves out."

She hoped so. "Shields, how much do you know about my friendship with Liz?"

"Whaddya mean?"

Priscilla shrugged and hoped it came across as nonchalant. "Just share whatever you know."

"Okay." He removed his hat and placed it next to the rifle. "I know she met you and Lola at the same time, at a party a long time ago. That the three of you have been good friends ever since. Like sisters."

Priscilla studied his face. His eyes didn't shift and his voice had stayed level when he'd talked about them meeting at a party. Did Liz not mention to him the *type* of party that they'd met at?

"What else do you know about Liz?"

He turned his face away from her and toward the hills in the distance. "I know she used to be an escort, if that's what you mean."

So he knew. "That is what I mean."

He whipped his face back toward her. "Mrs. King, if you're about to give me a lecture—"

"A lecture? On what?"

"On how I shouldn't be in a relationship with Liz."

She scoffed. "Shields, I'd be the last person to lecture you on that. How could I?"

His brows furrowed again. "I don't understand."

"Nevermind." Apparently, he was only aware of Liz's escorting history and not hers. "But I would like to know how you learned about Liz being an escort."

He rubbed the back of his neck. "The first night I took Liz to one of my games, a team member and former friend said horrible things about her. I decked him. A few of the other players then explained why he'd said those things."

So it hadn't been Liz who'd told him. It had come from others.

"Then I decked him again."

She jerked her head back. "You hit him again? Why?"

"Because it still didn't give him the right to talk about her that way."

"Does Liz know about the incident?"

He shook his head. "I'm not even sure she knows I know."

"She doesn't."

"That's what I don't get." He ran a hand through his dark curls. "We've become so close. I feel as though I've known her all my life. I've shared everything about my past with her—the good, the bad, and the ugly. She's shared tidbits with me, but I know there's a lot more to her story beyond the escorting. I know whatever happened to her as a child has wounded her. But being an escort? I don't understand why she won't open up to me about that."

"And it won't make a difference to you when she does?"

"No."

Priscilla hiked a brow.

"I'm telling you the truth. What I know, I've learned from others. I'd like to hear it from her. I don't want details. I just want her to know that she can tell me anything and that I'll still love her."

"And stay?"

His head jerked to the side. "Of course. Is there any other way to love someone?"

Was there? She didn't know. But it warmed her heart that he seemed to.

"You said you've told her everything about you. Does that include your time in prison?"

"Yep."

Wow. That was something else Liz hadn't bothered to tell her.

"You're wondering if I'm the right man for Liz."

"No. I think you're the perfect man for her. But even good men make promises they can't keep. I know there are no guarantees, but I just don't want to see Liz hurt. She's been through enough of that already. I'd like for the man she chooses to be her husband to add to her life, not take away from it."

"You're saying it takes a lot more than love?"

"I am. Especially with someone as fragile as Liz."

He returned his gaze to the hills.

"I'm also saying that before you say *'I do'* that you strongly consider not only everything Liz has been through, but if you'll be able to handle it."

He nodded, but didn't look her way.

"She's no longer an escort, but I've never known Liz to question the life she chose, but now she does. In the past, she's been very hesitant to talk about her childhood. Now she does. My point is that it takes Liz years to open up about deep, personal things. The two of you are set to get married next summer. What if, let's say, after five years of marriage, you find out something else about Liz? Something life-altering. Maybe for you, maybe for her. Either way, something like that would be hard to deal with in the best of marriages, let alone one that involved two strangers who rushed to the altar."

"You don't think I'm ready to get married?"

"I don't know you well enough to answer that question. What I am saying, is that it'll be wise to give Liz more time."

He shifted on the stone wall and looked at her. "What has Barry told you about me?"

Priscilla tilted her head. His tone wasn't defensive or angry, only inquisitive. Still, why had he asked that question? Had she unintentionally said or implied something she shouldn't have?

"He hasn't said much to me about you at all."

"So he has said something. What do you know?"

"I know that you're a hard-worker and that he trusts you to get things done when he's not around."

"Anything more … personal?"

"I obviously know you've been to prison, and why. I also know you previously had problems with alcohol."

"Did Barry tell you what led to me having issues with alcohol? Or why additional time was added to my prison sentence?"

Time had been added to his sentence? "No. Whatever you've said in confidence to Barry about those things, they've stayed in confidence."

He stared down at the wooden porch planks. "Well, let's just say that I'm no stranger to life-altering news or women who keep secrets. I didn't handle either of those situations well at the time, but I have learned from them." He looked up at her. "With God's help, there's nothing Liz can say to me now, five years from now, or even fifty years from now, that'll erode my love for her or cause me to leave her."

Priscilla was tempted to leave it there. She'd heard what she'd needed to hear—had *hoped* to hear. Liz needed someone with staying power, someone who wouldn't tuck tail and run when things got ugly.

Interestingly enough, it sounded like he needed someone like that, too.

But there was one more question she wanted to ask. Her selection process for the type of clients she'd entertained was a lot different from Liz's. Priscilla had only accepted clients who'd valued their privacy. The last thing she'd wanted was for her mom and sister to find out what she'd really been doing in her life at the time. And it had worked. Well, for the most part. There'd been rumors, of course, but Mama and Penelope weren't the type to listen to rumors. It wasn't until her ex, Jacob, went berserk, that Mama had learned the truth.

Liz, on the other hand, prioritized money over everything else. She didn't care about privacy because she wasn't ashamed of what she did.

Now that shamelessness had come back to haunt her.

Men who were always showing off how much money they had also talked a lot. About their money, their possessions, their women.

Some of that talk had reached the local baseball team. The Habakkuk Lions was a small, hometown team, not a professional one, but they had owners and investors with deep pockets.

The kind of clients Liz had looked for.

And Priscilla had avoided.

It was also likely the reason Shields had heard about Liz's exploits and not hers.

She blew out a breath. "Will the two of you be moving to Wyoming after you're married?"

He shook his head. "We're staying in Habakkuk."

Priscilla chewed her lip. She didn't want to cause a problem, but obviously they hadn't completely thought that through.

Shields cleared his throat. "I can tell you think that's a bad idea. And I don't know, maybe it is. But Liz and I have talked about this. She doesn't want to move away from you, Lola, or her other friends here. And she knows how much I love working here at the stables."

"People are going to talk."

"I know. But she doesn't seem to care about what people think of her."

"She doesn't. But that's not why I'm asking. What about you? Will *you* be able to handle the things other men may say about your wife? Without throwing punches? Because here in Habakkuk, that could end up being a whole lot of punches."

He looked at the sky. "*Without* throwing punches? Barry's helping me with that part. Will what they say affect how I feel about Liz? No."

She thought back to when she'd learned—from a friend, no less—that Barry's children had hired a private investigator. Then her thoughts fast-forwarded at warp speed to the humiliating scene between her and Grantham when she'd been out shopping. "Are you sure? Some people are relentless."

He looked her in the eyes and held her gaze. "I'm sure."

Priscilla nodded. "Thanks for taking the time to talk with me, Shields. It means a lot."

"Anytime." He stood, put on his hat and grabbed the rifle. "Will there be anything else, Mrs. King?"

She smiled. "Considering you're about to marry my best friend, whom I love like a sister, and someone Mama refers to as her daughter, I think it'll be okay if you call me Priscilla."

He chuckled and shook his head. "Uh, no ma'am. I won't be able to do that."

"Why not?"

"Barry, I mean Mr. King, he's okay with us referring to him either way, but when it comes to you, he insists that you're referred to only as Mrs. King."

"Really? Well, Mrs. King it is."

"Yes, ma'am."

He tipped his hat and headed toward the steps. Mama stepped onto the porch with a large stock pot that looked to weigh more than she did.

Shields slung the rifle over his shoulder and took the pot from her. "Miss Mabel, this pot is heavy. I could've come inside. Why didn't you text me to come get it?"

Mama had Shields' phone number? Wait. She texted? She'd always told her and Penelope that she didn't have time to learn that type of nonsense.

Mama wiped her hands on her blue-and-white checkered apron. "Prissy, don't start with me. Shields and the boys just showed me how to text the other day."

"Why are you yelling at me? I didn't say anything."

"You didn't have to. I knew what you were thinking. So stop it now."

Priscilla wanted to respond to the last part of that comment, but didn't dare. It'd be easier for her if she just changed her thought process than to be rebellious about it. She'd never been able to figure out as a child, a teen, or an adult how Mama always knew what she was thinking, but somehow she always did.

Shields carried the pot down the steps. "I'll run this over to the guys. Be right back."

Mama held up Priscilla's phone, which Priscilla had apparently left on the kitchen table. "No need. Barry called. He's around the corner. You boys go ahead and enjoy my turkey, potato, biscuit, and cheese soup while it's still hot."

"Will do. Thanks Miss Mabel."

When Shields got closer to the stables, Mama turned to her. "I could've answered all of those questions for you. You didn't have to bother Shields."

"I didn't just want answers, Mama. I wanted to see how he *reacted* to those questions. And it never hurts to talk directly to the source."

"Well, in that case, I'm glad you did. Liz means a lot to us. Besides, Shields needs to know from all of us how important she is to our family."

"How much of the conversation did you hear?"

Mama smiled.

"So all of it? Why didn't you just come out and join us?"

She opened the door. "I'm too busy. Got stuff to do."

Yeah, like texting Shields and the other *boys* in the stable.

"That'll be enough of that." Mama let the door slam behind her.

Priscilla chuckled. She ought to *text* Mama to apologize for her thoughts. And add Penelope to the message so that she, too, would know Mama had been keeping her new skill from them.

But somehow she didn't think Mama would find that funny.

Chapter 22

Priscilla followed Barry into his office and closed the door behind them.

He threw his brown leather jacket and gloves on the desk and laid his keys on top of them. "It's over."

"What's over?"

"The police know who tried to kill you."

Priscilla dropped into the chair across from his desk. She hoped it was the man in the woods and not Grantham. Barry's face wasn't giving her any clues.

"Who was it?"

"The man arrested today is Pharaoh Kaador. He's the guy the stable hands found roaming in the woods. He's from the New York area."

"Then what was he doing here?"

"Visiting Margaret."

Priscilla nodded. "So Mama was right. They know each other."

Barry sat on the corner of his desk. "According to him, they're more than friends."

"Grantham must be heartbroken."

"Heartbroken, but not innocent."

Priscilla stayed silent as Barry took in several deep breaths and cleared his throat twice before continuing. "Grantham hired two men to stalk and harass you, especially when you were in town. He'd planned to have them do that for several months. After that, he'd hoped you'd become so paranoid and irrational that it would create a wedge between us. Then he planned on introducing me to another woman."

Priscilla leaned on the desk. "What?"

"She'd been hired by him, too. Her role was to stir-up more strife and division between us, then disappear. His goal was to get us to divorce."

Priscilla opened her mouth to respond, then closed it. She repeated the process, but failed again. She wanted to say something, but for the life of her, the words wouldn't come out.

How *dare* he. Did Grantham think they'd be so easily manipulated? Broken apart?

And there was no way she would've tolerated being stalked and harassed for months. One, Barry never would've allowed it to go on that long, and two, neither would she. Those men weren't related to Barry. They weren't his children. She'd used kid gloves with Grantham and Victoria for that reason only. In her book, there were only two ways of handling bullies, and placating their abuse wasn't one of them.

Neither was being a victim.

Barry lowered his head. "I'm so sorry."

"For what?"

"My son's behavior."

"He's an adult. He started making his own decisions a long time ago."

"It's just that … I had no idea he was even capable of anything like this."

"And Mama had no idea I was capable of the things I did, either. But Barry, if there was hope for me, then there's definitely hope for Grantham."

"He sent people to harm you."

"And it didn't work. I'm still here. I survived the crash."

Barry blinked. "Oh, I forgot to tell you the rest of it."

"There's more?"

"Grantham hired the guys to harass you, not kill you. When he heard about what happened, he pulled the plug on the whole thing."

"So, they didn't mean to run me off the road?"

"They meant to. Margaret didn't like Grantham's plan. She told Pharaoh that her husband's plan would take too long, and she didn't think the two of us would walk away from each other, no matter what happened. She wanted a fool-proof plan. She wanted you dead."

Priscilla waited for an emotion to wave over her. Anger. Surprise. Shock. Disbelief. Nothing came. Perhaps a part of her had suspected Margaret in the first place.

Barry continued. "She went behind Grantham's back and paid the guys to crash into you and make it look like an accident. But like you said, they failed. She met Pharaoh a few years ago on one of her trips to New York. When you survived the crash, she asked him to finish the job."

"And that's why he was here on the estate?"

Barry nodded. "He thought he'd get a lay of the land. His plan was to come back later, hoping to catch you outside."

"And shoot me?"

"Yeah. But he knew I'd be here, along with several stable hands, and security. He was looking for a path where he'd be able to make a ninja-like escape. Especially since he wanted to exit the property unseen and free of bullet holes."

"But the guys caught him trespassing."

"Yep. Good news is, when he got to the station, he sang like a canary."

"Does Margaret know?"

"Yeah. They brought her in while I was still there."

"They arrested her?"

"They got her, Silly. The threat's over."

She smiled at his pet name for her. He hadn't used it in a while. That he was using it now showed he was breathing a little easier.

"Did she say anything to you?"

"Not to me, no. But she said a lot to the police. She denied everything and blamed it all on Grantham and Pharaoh. But they had proof of her involvement. Pharaoh showed the police tons of emails and text messages from her that told him what she'd wanted done and the best access points to our house from the back road. And Grantham had found a laptop she'd hidden above the ceiling tiles in one of the kid's bathrooms. His lawyer walked him into the station and they turned it in. Everything the police found on that computer was the smoking gun they needed."

"Wow."

"I know. Pharaoh also gave up the names of the guys in the hit-and-run. The New York police have them in custody."

"So, additional charges will now be added to Grantham."

"The charges against him are stacking up, but I'm so glad that attempted murder isn't one of them."

"So am I. And I'll help in any way I can."

She didn't like Grantham, and she knew the feeling was mutual. However, she loved his father, and whatever she could do to make his life easier, she would.

"That won't be necessary." He leaned toward her. "God and I have had a lot of conversations regarding Grantham. I'm at peace with letting the legal system handle it." He reached for her hand. "He's looking at some serious time, and I know you're worried about how that'll affect my relationship with him… but you have to remember, he's the one who started all of this."

"So Mama was right."

"She was."

Priscilla clasped his hand and kissed it. "Are you *truly* at peace? You're not just saying that for my sake?"

He shook his head. "I left everything out on the field that day."

"But today brought new challenges."

"It did, and I've surrendered them, too."

"The legal issues with Grantham could take a couple of years to get through. And then there's Victoria thinking she's communicating with her mom and—"

He squeezed her hand. "God's got Victoria and all the rest of it. I'm not saying it's going to be easy. It's going to be a lot, but… I guess the best way to put it is that I'm not stressed by any of it anymore."

"But if it does become too much, promise me you won't disappear into a field. That you'll come to me."

"I promise. I'll let you know, and we'll go before the Lord together. In the field."

She chuckled. "That's all I'm asking."

He pulled her out of her chair and into a hug. "But right now, I want you to leave."

"What?"

He smiled. "You've been cooped up in this house for weeks. I know you've been longing to get out. What do you want to do?"

She thought about that as she looked out of his office window. The sun had already set. Winter was definitely on the horizon. And so were the holidays. At least, she thought they were. She hadn't looked at a calendar in weeks.

"When's Thanksgiving?"

Barry lifted his wrist and tapped his watch. "Next week."

"What? Oh, my goodness. Are you serious?"

He smiled again. "Kind of lost track of time?"

"Apparently. I don't even know how that happened."

"Well, you were in the hospital for a couple of days.

Then recovered here, but the first week or two you were completely out of it because of the medication." He shrugged. "I can see how that could've happened."

"But no else has said anything about it. Not even Mama."

"Maybe she was waiting for you to bring it up? Would you like to do something for Thanksgiving?"

"I'd love to have a huge dinner. With Mama, my sister, Liz, Lola, my other girlfriends as well as Shields, the rest of the workers and their families."

Barry furrowed his brows. "Okay. But you do know—"

"I know. Thanksgiving's next week, and they probably have plans already."

Barry nodded. "Well, I know the workers already have plans with their families, but what about Mabel and Penelope?"

"Mama has hosted a Thanksgiving dinner for elderly seniors without loved ones for years. Last year, Eve let her use the café, so she'll probably do that again this year." Priscilla smiled. "But because they're older, a lot of them prefer an early dinner and like to return home before dark, so she's normally finished there before five o'clock. If you don't mind, we can have a small, intimate Thanksgiving here with family and a few friends. It'll be later in the evening, but I'd also like to invite Victoria and her family. And Grantham, if he's still out on bail."

"Victoria'll come if I ask. But I have no idea if Grantham will."

"Still, I'd like to extend the invite."

"Wouldn't that be a lot of cooking for Mabel? Seniors during the day and then cooking for us again that night?"

"For our dinner here, I'm going to cook."

"Mabel's not going to let you do that. You do know that our kitchen belongs to her now?"

"What?"

"She told me so. One morning, I tried to grab a quick bowl of cereal before heading out and she wouldn't let me. She said eating cold cereal in *her* kitchen was not allowed."

"She wouldn't let you eat?"

"Oh, I ate. She poured the cereal down the drain and made me a delicious bowl of oatmeal. And some sausage. And bacon, eggs, toast, and fresh-squeezed orange juice."

Priscilla giggled. "Figures. Did you know that she's also feeding your employees?"

"*Our* employees. And yes, I knew. I thought you did, too."

After all this time, she still had difficulty wrapping her mind around what was once only Barry's prior to them marrying, was now hers as well. "I didn't find out she was cooking for *our* employees until today. I just wanted to make sure that you knew and were okay with her doing so."

"I am. Are you?"

"Since it was her idea, I don't mind at all. And as far as Thanksgiving dinner is concerned, I'll talk with her about it. I don't think she'll mind. She knows I'm not an amateur in the kitchen. She taught me and my sister well."

"But it's been a while since you've cooked for anyone else but me. I mean," He pulled her closer. "I love the dinners for two you make just for us. Especially the one you made last Valentine's Day." His cheeks reddened. "How about we keep your *not* well-known cooking skills between the two of us?"

Their Valentine's Day meal had definitely been memorable. She'd prepared everything herself, without the help of Chef Rigalta, though she had him taste test everything. When he gave her the thumbs up, she knew she'd succeeded. But she and Barry both knew it wasn't the meal that had him blushing.

And he was right about her not having cooked a large meal in a while. Since they'd been married, it had been Chef Rigalta who'd prepared their holiday meals. Before Barry, when she was with Jacob, she hadn't cooked much either. Jacob was a huge fan of fine-dining and they ate out a lot. A *whole* lot. And their holiday meals were spent with the partners of his law firm, all of which had been catered.

She wanted to do this, but she didn't want to take anything special from Barry, either. "The only people who I think may join us are Ram, Lola, Liz, and hopefully, Shields. In addition to Mama and Penelope. That's just a handful of people. And my cooking skills aren't a secret to my family and girlfriends. It may be to Ram and Shields, though."

"May be?"

"The only way they'd know is if Lola or Liz told them. Lola talks a lot—about anything and everything—so I wouldn't be surprised if her husband knew. And apparently, Liz has done quite a bit of talking with Shields as well." She paused. She didn't want that last statement to get to her. At this point, Shields probably knew more about her friend than she did. And why hadn't Liz mentioned anything to her yet about getting married in Wyoming? Nevermind. She'd deal with those questions later. Right now, she wanted to focus on Thanksgiving. "Anyway, both of them may know already."

Barry sighed. "I'd still like for you to do something special for the two of us."

"Did you think I wouldn't?" She kissed him softly. "You're going to love what I have in mind."

He pulled her in for another kiss, seconds before Mama knocked on the office door.

"Prissy? Liz is here to see you."

Barry groaned.

"I'm sorry, love. But I think I know why she's here. And I *really* need to talk to her."

He slid off the desk and kissed her on the forehead. "That's all you're gonna get until you come back to me."

She giggled. "I won't be long, I promise."

At least she didn't intend to be away for long. She had

a lot on her mind.
	There was a lot she needed to get off her chest.
	With her so-called best friend.

Chapter 23

Priscilla stormed into the hearth room, where Liz was waiting for her. The morning's fire still blazed. Barry, Mama, or Rachel—the cleaning lady who came in twice a week—must have tended to it earlier.

Priscilla stopped in front of Liz. "I'm so angry with you right now. Why didn't you tell me you and Shields had already set a wedding date?"

Liz folded her arms across her chest. "How could you not tell *me it* was Margaret who was after you?"

"How could you possibly know that already?"

"Windy."

Priscilla tossed her hands in the air. Of course. Windy, a long-time friend of theirs, had seen her fair share of trouble, and was very familiar with the Habakkuk police and many of the station staff. She was no longer the girlfriend of a member of a local crime family, but she still had plenty of contacts in the police station. No doubt one of them saw Barry, Grantham, and Margaret there, and had called Windy to give her the scoop.

"Is that why you're here? To ask about Margaret?"

"Yes." Liz dropped her arms to the side. "And also to explain."

"About what? How you neglected to tell your best friend about the biggest day in your life?"

"Yes. Shields called and told me about the conversation you two had. He said he'd gotten the impression that the summer wedding and the trip to Wyoming were news to you."

"That's because it was."

"I know. The only two people in Habakkuk who knew about the wedding were me and Shields."

"Three."

"Three what?"

"Three people. Mama also knew."

Liz's eyes widened. "I don't know how that happened. I didn't mention anything to her about the wedding."

"Apparently, Shields did."

"Well, okay, three. But the reason I didn't want to tell you, Lola, or anyone else yet, is because I'm conflicted. I don't even know if I'll actually be able to go through with the wedding." She sighed. "Don't get me wrong, I love Shields. But I didn't want to say anything to anyone until I was sure of what I was going to do. Breaking Shields' heart will be devastating enough. I didn't want to break anyone else's.

Priscilla frowned. "I don't understand. All you've talked about the past couple of weeks is how excited you are to be his fiancé. So what has happened? Why the change of heart?"

"It's not like that. What I'm saying is that I *want* to marry him. I just don't know if I *should*."

"What do you mean?"

"I'm broken, Pris. You know that."

"Liz—"

"I scheduled the wedding for next summer because I can't wait to begin my life with him. We've set it for August

5, almost nine months away. That's enough time for a child to be conceived and born.

"I thought about what you said regarding Ruth Greene and the group she runs. I called your church the other day and got the chance to speak with her. She's given me a lot of hope. And I've agreed to go to the meetings. But if I can't be fixed in nine months—the same amount of time it takes for a new life to form—then I'm unfixable. I love Shields too much to have him commit to my broken world. He's an awesome guy and deserves so much more than I'll ever be able to give him."

"And you think standing him up at the altar is the answer?"

"That's the last thing I'd want to do, but I also want to give myself every opportunity to get better. Up to the very last second."

Priscilla took Liz's elbow and led her to the couch, even though she wasn't in the mood for sitting. She was better at arguing when she was standing. And she was still angry. No. She was hurt. Why hadn't Liz shared those details with her earlier? She understood Liz's reasoning, but it still hurt.

When they were seated, she asked, "If Shields wasn't going to know until the very last minute, when were you planning on telling the rest of us that a wedding was even going to take place?'"

"About a month or two before."

"Are you serious? That's all the time you were going to give us? Oh, and let's not forget that you're getting married in Wyoming. And that I'm apparently supposed to travel there, meet his family, and help you, his mom, and his sister find a wedding venue."

"Yeah. Like I said, a month or two before."

Priscilla sucked in a breath. Either she wasn't communicating effectively, or Liz was intentionally being obstinate and refusing to see her point.

But what was her point?

Yes, she'd been hurt by Liz not sharing information about the wedding sooner. But Liz had already explained that. Priscilla hadn't liked her answer, but it was an explanation. An explanation she'd understood. So, why was she still picking at stuff that didn't matter?

Jealousy.

There was a part of her that was jealous that Shields had known about the wedding details and she hadn't.

Which was crazy, because he was her fiancé. Of course, he should've known. But she felt left out. She would've loved to have helped Liz plan her wedding. That's what friends did. But Liz had left her out of it.

She rubbed the back of her neck. She could sit here and continue to nurse that wound and hound Liz for more answers—answers that'd just be variations of the ones Liz had already given—or she could focus on what really mattered.

Her friend.

Liz had given herself a timeline of nine months to go from broken to fixed. And if that deadline wasn't met, she was going to walk away from one of the best things that had ever happened to her—love.

What kind of friend would Priscilla be if she sat back and let that happen?

Lord, I can't believe how petty I'm being right now. My friend is sitting next to me hurting and all I can do is think about myself. Forgive me.

Priscilla cleared her throat. "Liz, if you love Shields, I think you should marry him regardless of how you feel in nine months."

"What? Why would I do that?"

"Because Shields loves you."

"Being married to me could bring him a life full of misery, Pris."

"Or it could bring him a life full of happiness."

"You're not hearing me."

"I hear you loud and clear, and what I'm hearing is that you don't have enough faith in your fiancé. Today was the first time I had the chance to have a one-on-one conversation with him, and I was impressed. Also, I've been here three years and I've yet to hear anyone say anything bad about him. In fact, it's been just the opposite. He's Barry's top hand for a reason. And you know Barry, he focuses on a person's character, not the compliments they receive. The fact that he trusts him to run this place when he's not around says a lot. And then there's Mama."

Liz swallowed. "Please don't tell me she had a vision about Shields."

Priscilla chuckled. "No, she hasn't. But unlike Barry, she doesn't let someone's character make a decision for her when it comes to people. You and I both know she has great discernment. And she's discerned that Shields not only has a good heart, but a good spirit. She adores him."

Liz's eyes watered.

"And he knows more about you, Liz, than you realize."

Her eyes widened. "No."

"Yes. He knows everything. One of his teammates had teased him about you. And Shields is still here for you, Liz. He didn't freak out, he didn't run away. Heck, he didn't even get mad. Well, not at you. His teammate… well, let's just say he won't be teasing Shields about you anymore."

"What happened?"

"He punched the guy. Twice."

"Oh, no. He didn't go to jail, did he? One arrest and you're off the team. He loves playing for the Lions. The last thing I'd want is to ruin that for him."

"Well, he's still on the team, so everything's fine."

Liz let out a shaky breath and tears flowed down her face. She wiped them with the back of her hand and smiled.

"You okay?"

"You said he punched the guy?"

Priscilla nodded.

"That's the first time in my entire life," she wiped at a new flow of tears. "That a man has stood up for me. Defended me. Thought I was *worth* defending."

"Oh, Liz."

"I know it sounds awful, but I feel kinda giddy. You're sure he didn't say anything about getting into trouble with the team?"

"He didn't."

She bobbed her head back and forth. "Good. Good."

"He did say that he'd wished he'd heard it from you first, though. He was also concerned. He wondered why you didn't trust him enough to tell him."

Liz lowered her eyes.

Priscilla lowered her head to look into those eyes. "Listen, when Shields finds out that I shared that with you, he'll probably never confide in me again. He may never even *talk* to me again because that wasn't my story to tell. It was his. I'm breaking that confidence because I need you to know just how much you mean to him, Liz. Broken or fixed."

Liz leaned in closer. "How do you deal with it?"

She'd said it so softly that Priscilla had to read her lips to understand what she'd said.

"How do I deal with what?"

"The shame."

Priscilla straightened and tightened her lips before the phrase, "*what shame*", thoughtlessly spilled out of them. She didn't have to ask Liz what she'd meant. She already knew.

Her mind went to one of her favorite passages in the Bible, the one where it talked about the woman caught in adultery. Angry men had dragged her across the ground and took her to Jesus. The Law demanded that she be stoned. And the men had looked forward to pelting her with them.

Killing her with them.

She'd been caught in the very act. There was no denying her guilt.

Priscilla had often wondered what thoughts had gone through the woman's mind as she was dragged down dusty roads and thrust into the crowd. Had she been angry? Angry at the men who'd caught her red-handed? Angry that she'd be the only one to face punishment? What about the man she was with? Was he going to get away scot-free?

Or had she been embarrassed? Everyone in the crowd surrounding Jesus now knew what she'd done in secret. Did she want to apologize to the man's wife? To Jesus? Did she long to scream out that she'd never do it again?

Or had she looked forward to the first stone?

The degradation. The guilt.

The shame.

Had it been too much? Unbearable? Would she have rather died than to continue to have her deeds exposed to the masses?

Had she craved the pain of the stones? So that she'd be able to feel anything, everything but … shame?

But the stones never came.

Jesus had written on the ground, spoken to the men, and they'd left.

No one had remained there except her and Jesus.

He then asked her, *"Woman, where are those your accusers?"*

She'd replied, *"No man, Lord."*

And Jesus had said unto her, *"Neither do I condemn you: go, and sin no more."*

Whether or not the woman knew at the time that Jesus would actually keep the Law and pay the penalty by dying in her place, Priscilla didn't know.

But she did remember what God had said to her when she'd heard Pastor Greene teach on that Scripture.

Unashamed.

Before she'd married, she'd struggled with the same issues Liz was struggling with now. Oh, how she'd wished she could've done things differently. She would've given anything to have been able to present herself pure to Barry.

But she wasn't. She was the exact opposite of that.

But the sermon had raised a lot of questions for her. She'd wanted to know more, to dive deeper into the woman caught in the act of adultery.

And her friends, Lydia and Eve, helped her do that.

She'd learned that when she'd accepted Christ as her Savior, she'd been made brand new.

Just like those babies Liz had talked about earlier.

And because of what He'd done for her on the Cross, Priscilla had been able to present her best self to Barry.

Unashamed.

Just like God had whispered to her that Sunday morning in church.

She wanted to explain all of that to Liz, but knew her friend well enough to know she'd need to take baby steps. And right now, all Liz wanted to know was how she'd dealt with the shame.

"I didn't deal with it. Jesus did."

Liz scoffed. "According to you, Ruth, and Lola, Jesus did a lot of amazing things."

"He did. And He still does."

Liz fell back against the couch and folded her arms again. "You're not giving me real answers."

"They're more real than you know. And you want to know what else? I think the reason you've been fighting so hard against getting to know Jesus is because He's calling you to be closer to Him."

"You're speaking a foreign language."

"I know, and Ruth'll be able to translate a lot better than I can. But right now, as your friend, I want you to know that I think you'll be making a huge mistake even thinking about walking away from Shields. Extend the wedding to August of next year if necessary. Be willing to give yourself all the time you need. There's no rush."

"Next year is a long way away, Pris. And I'm tired of

being lonely."

"But you'll be lonely anyway if you're not *fixed,* as you put it. You would've left Shields at the altar because you wouldn't have wanted to drag him into your misery."

"You're acting like I have a choice in this. I've lived in misery. I don't want anyone going through that. I love Shields, and I'd like for him to have the chance to find real happiness."

"So you've already decided for him? You're not even going to ask him how he feels about it? You're just going to blindside him at the altar? Or before? That's not love, Liz."

Liz shook her head. "I don't want to talk about this anymore, Pris. I only stopped by because I wanted to explain and apologize for hurting you." She straightened. "I am so sorry I didn't tell you about my wedding plans next summer. And no matter how I try to spin it, there's simply no excuse for not telling you. When Shields told me about the hurt he saw in your eyes, I knew I had to come right away. I never meant to hurt you. Please know that."

Priscilla blinked away tears. "I know." She pulled Liz into a hug. "And I apologize for coming on so strong. I know you're struggling with a lot of emotions right now. I should've been more understanding."

Liz chuckled in her ear. "You're a lot more understanding than I would've been. If I'd found out from someone else that you and Barry were getting married, I would've cried a river that rivaled the size of the one behind your house. Then I would've spray painted your wedding dress."

"What color?"

"Turquoise."

Priscilla laughed loudly and pulled away. "You wouldn't!"

"Oh, I would've."

Priscilla hated the color turquoise. Despite the fact that stylists everywhere insisted that everyone looked good in turquoise, she knew different. She looked horrid in that color.

Liz glanced at her watch and stood. "I've gotta scoot. Shields is waiting for me."

"Outside?"

"No. At Rosco's."

Rosco's was a local burger joint that had been in Habakkuk for almost fifty years. "What are you two doing for Thanksgiving?"

"Not sure. Neither one of us has any plans, so maybe frozen dinners in front of the TV? Why do you ask?"

"I'd like to host Thanksgiving dinner here. It'll be later in the evening, though, after Mama and Penelope are done working at the diner. I'd love for you and Shields to come."

"I'd love that, and I know Shields would too, but let me ask." She pulled her phone from her purse and typed out a text. When it dinged, she laughed and showed Shields' response to Priscilla. He'd sent a dancing cowboy emoji with three thumbs up underneath it. "I think you can consider that a yes."

"Awesome. Hopefully, Ram and Lola will join us as well. I'll call later with the details."

She hugged Liz again when they reached the door, then watched her get in the car and drive away. She loved her friend and was glad that she'd stopped by. And Liz's apology was a balm to Priscilla's wounded heart.

But right now, she had unfinished business to tend to.

She locked the door and headed back to Barry's office.

Time to return to her husband and finish what they'd started earlier.

Chapter 24

Black Friday.

Though it wasn't an official holiday, it was on Priscilla's calendar.

She took one last look in her bedroom mirror. Her hair had actually cooperated this morning and was continuing to hold its naturally wavy style without the use of hairspray.

Then there was the scar.

The gash. A stark reminder that her step-daughter-in-law had tried to kill her.

Earlier, she'd attempted using concealer to camouflage the deep rive in her forehead, but the concealer actually made the scar look worse. And when she'd added makeup on top of it, the scar looked like it was protruding out of her forehead. She needed Liz. Her friend was skilled in making the darkest circles, deepest wrinkles, blotches, and blemishes of all sizes disappear, with a swoop of her diamond-accented makeup brush, and her homemade miracle cream in a jar.

Priscilla groaned. She'd just have to wait and have Liz fix the scar when she saw her later this evening.

Or maybe not.

Maybe she should wear the scar proudly.

Not as a reminder of what Margaret had tried to do to her, but as a reminder that by the grace of God and His mercy, she'd failed.

She touched the scar. It was no longer bright red or tender, and Dr. Greengold had removed the stitches weeks ago, but it was still rough to the touch. And long. It started at the tip of her left brow and curved past her left temple toward her cheek. It had the width of a worm.

Priscilla smiled and stepped away from the mirror. The scar was ugly and very noticeable. Good. Maybe that would prompt people to ask her about it, then she'd be able to tell them all about the goodness of God.

Her friend Eve evangelized to nearly everyone she came across and did it without the need of a prompt. Priscilla wasn't quite that bold yet, but if her scar started that type of conversation, she wasn't going to shy away from it.

She slid on a pair of her favorite boots. They were a festive red and perfect for the upcoming Christmas season. The three-inch heel was a must-have. Today, she wasn't going to bother with any heel shorter than that. They were boring. It had been over a month since she'd been able to meet up with friends. She was healthy, alive, and full of energy. There was no room in her life today for boring.

She stepped into the hallway, walked to the stairs, and stopped when she heard laughter, followed by Mama's and Chef Rigalta's voices.

The stairs ended near the kitchen, so they were obviously in there. But why?

When they'd found out Margaret was denied bail, Mama had returned to sleeping in her own home. On Monday, she was scheduled to resume her work at the café, and Chef wasn't to return to his job here until Monday as well.

Yet, they were both in the kitchen. Together.

And when was the last time she'd heard Mama laugh

like that?

There weren't many times Priscilla regretted wearing heels, but this was one of them.

Lord, please forgive me in advance for the reckless act I'm going to attempt. Help me go down these stairs without tumbling and breaking my neck. My heels against the wood will alert Mama to my presence. I know it's sneaky, but Lord, You know if I ask Mama what she and Chef were laughing about, she won't tell me. So I have to do it this way.

Okay. She didn't *have* to. She had a choice.

She blew out a shaky breath and decided to spy on Mama.

She grabbed both handrails in a death grip, then slowly toed her way to the first landing, using the tips of her feet only.

She'd made it. *Thank you, Lord.*

Leaning her back against the wall, she cupped her ear to listen in on Mama's and Chef's conversation.

Nothing.

Back still against the wall, she peeked around it into the kitchen. They were both still there. Mama was wiping down the counters and Chef Rigalta was removing dishes from one cabinet and placing them into another.

Priscilla's chest tightened. They moved around each other like they'd done it many times before. Like a married couple that had danced the same dance for decades.

Daddy used to move around Mama like that.

She remembered watching through young eyes how Daddy would reach for Mama's hand and give her a twirl right there in the middle of their tiny little kitchen. She and Penelope would giggle quietly from the small makeshift dinner table, as their parents danced around the kitchen to no music.

Priscilla wiped away a tear. She missed Daddy.

If Chef Rigalta reached for Mama's hand, what would she do? Soft instrumental music flowed through the kitchen speakers, so it was a possibility.

Would Mama give Chef her hand? If she did, would that mean they were dating?

Priscilla didn't know how she'd feel about that.

She also didn't know how it could be possible. Chef Rigalta prepared high-end fare with ingredients she doubted most Americans pronounced properly. Mama was a home cook who used ingredients everybody loved, but Chef Rigalta despised.

Mama had also led Priscilla to believe that she didn't care much for Chef Rigalta or his cooking.

And she'd never forget the day when Chef told Mama that her cooking lacked style and creativity.

Priscilla had to grab Mama's elbow and usher her outside, which wasn't an easy feat. Mama was small, but she was strong, and she had a lot to say to the man who'd continued to add insult to injury by saying Mama would benefit greatly from a course in the culinary arts.

Mama then grabbed a wooden rolling pin and swung it at him. Priscilla used the momentum from the swing to push Mama out the door.

Priscilla wondered if Chef knew that she'd saved his life that day.

The way they worked around each other today, though, smiling intermittently, it was hard to imagine that day had ever happened.

Despite Mama's behavior, she never would've been the first one to issue an apology. Perhaps it was Chef Rigalta who'd extended the olive branch?

He could've. He was arrogant when it came to cooking, but Priscilla had found him to be quite gentlemanly and kind when food wasn't the topic of the conversation. Had Mama found him to be that way also?

That stung. Daddy passed away decades ago, but Priscilla still preferred to think that Mama only had eyes for him.

She jerked her head back behind the wall. Had Grantham and Victoria felt the same way about their mom and dad?

Did they have cherished memories of their parent's being together also? Wonderful memories that turned painful after Priscilla arrived on the scene?

What if everything they'd said, did, and had intended to do to her wasn't about money after all? What if it was about memories?

She resisted the urge to run her fingers through her hair. She didn't have time to tiptoe back up the stairs to fix it.

And she didn't have time to waste on Victoria's and Grantham's feelings, either.

Despite how she'd feel if Mama and Chef really were in a relationship, she'd never do anything hateful or criminal.

Would she?

Priscilla waved away the question. She'd delve into that later. Maybe. She had more important things to figure out.

For instance, she knew Mama's marital status, but she didn't know Chef Rigalta's. Was he divorced? Separated? Or widowed like Mama?

There was also the chance that he was married.

No. She'd known him for three years, and Barry had known him for decades. Neither of them had ever heard Chef mention a wife.

She knew from the employee files in Barry's office that Chef was a year older than Mama. She'd also read he was born and raised in Italy, attended culinary school, and worked in several homes as a private chef in Milan before arriving in America to work for a family on the west coast. Years later, he was hired by Barry's family.

She'd also seen that he had four adult sons, all of whom were listed as emergency contacts. But for the life of her, she couldn't remember what box he'd checked under marital status.

She took another peek around the corner. Mama was

only five-three. Priscilla didn't know Chef's height, but he towered over her. Just like Daddy had.

She'd heard from friends that Mama had dated some after Priscilla left for college, but nothing ever came of those dates. She hadn't had a significant relationship since Daddy, and he'd passed away when Priscilla was twelve.

"How long you gonna stand there and look at us, Prissy?"

Priscilla lowered her head. Busted.

She walked down the remaining steps and into the kitchen. "Good morning."

They replied with the same greeting. At the same time. She gritted her teeth. Why did that bother her so?

Mama pressed a narrow hip against the counter. "Where are you going?"

Priscilla glanced at the kitchen clock above the pantry. "Windy's picking me up in about twenty minutes. We're going shopping."

Mama and Chef both turned toward the stove. "Let us fix you something." Chef turned to Mama, and they both laughed when they realized they'd said the exact same thing. Again.

Priscilla wasn't amused. "That's okay. If she gets here on time, we might stop by the café before heading out. By the way," she focused on Chef Rigalta. "Weren't you supposed to be there this morning?"

He nodded. "I was."

Priscilla narrowed her eyes. "Wouldn't today be quite busy for the café? I imagine people would like to eat before and after going shopping."

He chuckled. "Of course. We had a line waiting outside the doors when we opened at five a.m. No worries, though. I didn't abandon Eve. She's in good hands."

"You and Mama are here, so I don't understand."

Mama lifted the tea kettle off the stove and filled it with water. "You remember Hyman Moe?"

Priscilla tilted her head to the side. Why did that name sound familiar?

"He's the one who was friends with that guy who tried to kill Kite."

Priscilla took a step back. Kite was Windy's twin sister. And Priscilla definitely remembered Tyler, and how he'd tried to kill both Kite and her cousin, Gypsy. She also remembered when he'd burned down Kite and her husband, Jack's home. Hyman Moe had been a close friend of Tyler's.

Her heart picked up it's pace. "What does Hyman Moe have to do with you and Chef Rigalta?"

"Carlo has been training him to become a chef."

Carlo was Chef Rigalta's first name. She bit her lip. They were on a first name basis now?

Mama placed the kettle on the stove. "I know what you're thinking. Let me explain before you throw a hissy fit."

"Yes, Mama. Please explain."

"Hyman Moe was friends with Tyler, yes. But Hyman never hurt Kite or anyone else in her family. If you remember correctly, he was shot several times for being in the park with Tyler."

"What?"

"He was—"

"I know what Hyman Moe was doing there, Mama. That's not what I thought you were going to explain."

Mama's brows furrowed. "Are you fully awake, Prissy? What else would there be for me to explain?"

Priscilla rolled her shoulders back and forth. The tension in them threatened to crawl up the back of her neck. She'd thought Mama was going to explain her and Chef Rigalta's, or should she say *Carlo's* new friendship. Or was it a relationship? Either way, Mama didn't think there was anything to explain.

She wasn't going to push it. Not today. "Nevermind, Mama." She blew out a breath. "You were talking about

Hyman Moe?"

"He served time for having an illegal weapon, but now he's out on probation. He was blessed by Ruth Greene's prayers for him when he was in the hospital. He'd promised when he got out of jail he'd find a good church. And he did, and it's really close to the café. Eve had a help wanted sign in the window, and that's when he met Carlo."

Carlo.

Priscilla scratched at her forehead and winced when a fingernail cut across the scar.

This day was not starting out the way she'd hoped.

Far from it.

Chapter 25

Priscilla yanked open the passenger door to Windy's Mazda and plopped into the seat.

"Thanks for rescuing me."

Windy smiled that sly smile of hers. "You and Barry have a bad morning?"

"Nothing like that. It's Mama."

"You and Miss Mabel get into a fight?"

"Yes… no. I'm fighting with her. She just doesn't know it."

"Mabel knows everything."

"I think Mama and Chef Rigalta are dating."

Windy scoffed. "Yeah, right."

"I don't know for sure, but I definitely suspect it." She turned in her seat. Windy's hair was in its usual ponytail. Normally, it was kept in place with dark-colored holders and ties that blended into the blackness of her hair. Today, though, her ponytail was tied with a green hair ribbon with candy canes on it. The ribbon followed the length of her hair, which went past her shoulders and matched her usual attire—an athletic suit. However, the athletic attire she usually wore was more on the trendy side. This one, unfortunately, matched her ribbon perfectly.

"Well… um, don't you look… Christmasy."

"Don't laugh. Anthony's mother saw this suit and for some crazy reason thought I'd like it. I hate it. I look like an idiot. Worse. I look like an idiot who loves candy canes."

Anthony was Windy's boyfriend. They'd been together longer than she and Barry had been married. Priscilla was sure he was going to pop the question any day now, and apparently, so was Windy. Why else would she willingly wear that comical outfit?

Priscilla placed a hand over her mouth, but it was of no use. She couldn't stop laughing. "Windy," she gasped for breath between bursts of laughter. "If you hate it, why in the world are you wearing it?"

"Because I promised his mom I would. She's going to be out shopping today as well. I wanted her to see me in it in case we run into her. Show her I'm a woman of my word."

Priscilla held her stomach and continued to gasp for air. "Trying to impress the future mother-in-law?"

"Yes, I am." She reached into her candy cane-themed jacket and pulled out a pair of earrings and dropped them into Priscilla's hand. "This is where I draw the line, though. Aren't those the most hideous earrings you've ever seen?"

Priscilla lifted one of the earrings. It dangled in front of the windshield in all of its candied glory. Not only were the earrings designed with tiny little candy canes separated by thin strands of gold—they also sported colorful little gum drops.

"Believe it or not, Wind, I've seen worse."

"No way."

"Oh, yeah."

"I don't want to wear them. Do you think she'll notice?"

"Yep."

She took the earrings and put them on. "And you thought *you* were having a bad day."

"Well, my friend, I want you to know that you've officially made it better."

Windy gave her a toothy smile. "I'm here to please."

Priscilla blew out a breath. "Wind?"

"Uh oh. Your tone just went from light to heavy. This must be serious."

Was it? She didn't know. But she also didn't want Windy or her twin sister blindsided either.

"Did you know that Hyman Moe was working at Kay's Café?"

Windy started the car and the turbo engine roared. "Yeah. We know."

Thank goodness. Priscilla would've hated to be the first one to drop a bomb like that. "How does Kite feel about him working there?"

"You know Kite. She's all about second chances. Me? Not so much. But before Eve hired him, she met with his parole officer and the pastor of his new church. They all said they believe he's a changed man. Those meetings, along with everything Ruth and Pastor Greene shared about him, helped Eve feel more at ease about hiring him."

"Do you guys think it was a good idea?"

"Kite loves the idea. But remember, I've known Hyman Moe a long time. Way before his near-death experience, so my opinion on his new found faith is jaded. But God has given me tons of second chances and so have my friends and family. I'm just hoping he doesn't disappoint everyone."

Windy pulled out of the driveway. Priscilla adjusted her seat and pulled the seatbelt tight across her white, oversized sweater. She'd never personally met Hyman Moe, but she was still surprised to hear that he worked at the café.

Not only did he work there, he was being trained by Chef Rigalta.

Hyman Moe had been given a second chance.

So had she, and so had Windy.

They were the poster girls for second chances. Like

Hyman Moe, they weren't worthy of their second chances, but they were given to them, anyway.

But what about people like Mama? People who were good, honest, ethical, moral, and who genuinely tried to avoid trouble rather than run towards it? Okay, the last part she couldn't actually ascribe to Mama, but not once in Mama's seventy-six years had she dated a known criminal like Windy, slept with men she wasn't married to, like herself, or served time in prison like Hyman.

Were there second chances for them?

Or were they living the "good" life in vain?

"You okay, Pris?"

She nodded and looked out the passenger window. "Yeah, just thinking."

When Windy turned on Logton Road, Priscilla closed her eyes. The hill that her car had tumbled down, just a few short weeks ago, was coming up. When she and Barry had gone grocery shopping for Thanksgiving, he'd intentionally taken an alternate route, and she'd been grateful. She wasn't ready to see the spot where her life had almost ended.

Talk about second chances.

Daddy had always talked about how everyone needed Christ the Savior. The young and the old, the good and the bad. The innocent and the guilty.

Good people needed a Savior, but did they need second chances from their loved ones? She doubted it. Good people had nothing to prove, and they didn't have to worry about rumors, bad reputations, or people wondering if they were worthy of their trust. Or their love.

Love.

That's what was bothering her. Daddy loved Mama. Priscilla remembered how his eyes danced along with every muscle in his body as he'd held Mama close and glided across the old but gleaming, honey-colored parquet flooring.

And Mama had loved Daddy, too. The sorrow in Mama's voice when she couldn't wake Daddy on that long ago Sunday afternoon had told Priscilla just how much.

That Mama could possibly *love* another bothered Priscilla. Mama was a young woman when Daddy died and was now well into her golden years. Surely, she deserved a second chance at being just as happy as she'd been with Daddy.

But Priscilla wondered if she'd be able to give her one.

Windy turned onto a narrow highway that would eventually dump them close to downtown Habakkuk. "Is it Hyman Moe you're thinking about or Mabel?"

"Both. Along with love and second chances."

"Love? You think Miss Mabel is in love?"

Priscilla shrugged. "I don't know. If they were, would that be a bad thing?"

"Of course not. There's no such thing as too much love."

Priscilla turned toward Windy. "Who are you and what have you done with my friend?"

Windy chuckled. "Let's just say I've learned a lot about love over the past couple of years." Windy's phone dinged and she pointed to the cup holder between them, where it sat. "Do you mind reading that text for me? It's probably from my crazy future-mother-in-law wondering why she hasn't run into us yet."

Priscilla tapped open the message. "It's from her. How do you want me to reply?"

"Ask where she's at and tell her we'll meet up with her there."

Priscilla typed out the message. The phone dinged again.

"Where is she?"

Priscilla stared at the name of the store. Could this day hold any more surprises?

"She's at Prophet's."

"Oh." Windy paused, then said. "Listen Pris, we don't have to go there. She's probably getting gifts for her husband

and sons. Just let her know we'll meet up somewhere else later this afternoon."

Prophet's Fine Jewelry was one of Priscilla's favorite places to shop for Barry. But Grantham had ruined that the day he'd humiliated her in front of the store's employees. The looks on their faces when he'd called her names she didn't want to think about, let alone repeat.

The shock on hers when he'd stomped the watch she'd just purchased for Barry with his black wing-tipped leather shoes.

The hatred in his eyes. The disdain in theirs—for her.

She'd known the employees for years. Each one of them by name. They'd known hers, too. Now she wondered if they'd only remember her by the ones Grantham had called her, especially since one of them had also begun with the letter, P.

His slurs. Their stares. Patrons backing away from her like she had the plague. She couldn't go back there. How could she?

Windy elbowed her. "For the record, I think we should go. Not because Anthony's mom is there, but because you have nothing to be ashamed of. Grantham was the one who acted a fool in the store that day, not you."

"You didn't see their faces."

"Didn't have to, because it doesn't matter. *He's* the one who should feel embarrassed, not you."

Priscilla ran her fingers through her hair. Blast it.

She pulled down the visor and looked into the lighted mirror. Not too much damage. The last thing she wanted to do was use a holding product on her hair. It would hold her natural style, but it wouldn't remain as soft or continue to sway with ease. She'd dodged a bullet. This time. Her hair was temperamental, which is why her purse had everything she'd need in case of an emergency. Or did it? She reached for her purse.

Windy nudged her again before she could grab it. "I'm

not going to let you *primp* your way out of answering me, Pris. Reply to that text right now and tell her we'll be there in ten minutes. You still need to purchase that watch you wanted to buy for Barry. And you're going to walk in there as proud as a peacock to do it—even if I have to drag you over the threshold first."

Chapter 26

Windy swung open the door to Prophet's Fine Jewelry.

The Christmas song *Joy To World* enveloped them.

Priscilla thought she would've been hesitant to step into the store again, but Windy was right. She'd done nothing wrong. And if questions arose, she'd do her best to explain. She'd once thought of the store owners and their employees as friends. She'd hoped they'd thought of her the same way, too.

She sucked in a breath. She'd find out one way or the other shortly.

When it came to square footage, Prophet's wasn't a huge store. But the expert placement of mirrors, shelving, and glass booths made it appear much larger than it was. And apparently, there was a sale going on, because the place was packed.

They walked toward the glass case that contained men's watches. Priscilla immediately recognized one that was close in design to the one she'd intended to buy Barry. The price was steeper, but it had additional elements Barry would enjoy. She looked around for an associate, but they were all helping other customers.

"I think I'm going to get this one."

Windy looked into the case. "Is that the one you were initially going to get him?"

"No. Grantham smashed that one to smithereens. I doubt they still have it, but I think he'd like this one, too."

Priscilla felt a tap on her shoulder and turned around. Two young women, both with long, brunette hair and bright smiles, stared at her. The one with blue eyes was Ashley, and the one with brown eyes was Meg—both associates of the store who'd she'd always loved to work with, and whom she'd considered friends. They were also the two who'd looked at her differently after Grantham's stunt.

Meg stepped closer to her. "Priscilla, we're so glad you're here. We weren't sure if we'd ever see you again."

Priscilla swallowed. They'd *wanted* to see her again?

Ashley nodded. "We were horrified by what happened to you that day. I've never seen anyone treat someone like that. It was horrible."

Meg's cheeks reddened. "I had nightmares for days after that. I hope to never see that man again. Ever."

Windy handed her a tissue. Priscilla stared at it for a moment before taking it. She dabbed at her cheeks. She hadn't even felt her eyes water, let alone spill over. She looked at the moistened tissue. Apparently, they had.

Priscilla cleared her throat. "I don't …" She cleared it again after those two words came out in a croak. "I don't know what to say. I didn't think either of you would want anything to do with me after that day."

Meg furrowed her brows. "Why?"

"The look on your faces … I don't know. Grantham had said a lot of awful things and—"

"It was *his* actions we were reacting to, not yours."

Windy coughed. Priscilla knew she didn't have a cold. That was Windy's way of reminding her she'd been right.

Grantham was the one that had made a scene, not her.

Priscilla looked into Meg's and Ashley's eyes. "I'm sorry. I immediately thought the worse. You two didn't deserve that. I'm the one who needs to apologize to you."

"Nothing to apologize for." Ashley pulled Priscilla into a hug and squeezed her tight. Meg joined in. "We've missed you."

"I've missed you, too."

Ashley stepped out of the hug. "And just so you know, Carol and Davis banned Grantham and his wife permanently from the store, so you don't have to worry about anything like that happening again."

Carol and Davis Glenn were the owners. Priscilla glanced around the store. "Are they here? I'd like to thank them, though the ban won't be necessary. Grantham and his wife are headed to prison."

Their eyes widened.

Priscilla chuckled. "Long story and it looks like you ladies are swamped. How about I stop by again after the holiday rush? We could do lunch."

They agreed. Priscilla pointed to the watch. "Today, though, I'd like to buy that for Barry before someone else snatches it up."

Meg tilted her head to the side. "You don't want the one you originally picked out?"

"Grantham crushed it with his heel. The Glenn's probably had to write it off as a loss."

"No. Davis was able to repair it." She dashed around the case. "Ashley, that lady in front of the necklace display is waving at us. You take care of her and I'll grab the watch."

Meg disappeared into the back and Windy grabbed Priscilla's arm. "That lady is Anthony's mom." She headed toward the necklace display with Ashley. "Come over after you get the watch, and I'll introduce you."

Priscilla nodded and Meg reappeared with a black leather watch box and opened it. She couldn't believe it. It was as though the damage had never even occurred.

"Oh, my goodness. It's beautiful."

"It is, isn't it? Davis is an amazing jeweler. He's fixed tons of pieces that people thought were beyond repair."

Meg then wrapped the watch box in silver and black gift wrap before placing it in one of the highly coveted Prophet's gift bags. The two-handle bags, black, and emblazoned with the word *Prophet's* in gold across the front, were a symbol of luxury in small town Habakkuk.

Priscilla reached into her purse and Meg shook her head. "Carol told all the associates that if you were to come back into the store, we were to let you know this one would be on the house."

Priscilla gasped. "That can't be right. The watch is over a thousand dollars, not to mention the repair costs."

"The Glenns were very upset that security didn't respond sooner to their calls for help. She said, this is their way of apologizing for what happened, and not having a system in place to stop it."

"Where are they?"

"Out of town. They'll be back at noon tomorrow."

Priscilla blinked back a fresh set of tears. This was not what she'd expected when she walked through those doors. She'd expected vitriol and hatred, but had received the exact opposite.

"Then I'll be back tomorrow. I'd like to thank them in person for their generosity and kindness."

"I'll leave them a message. They'll be excited to see you again.

"Thank you, Meg. For everything."

"You're welcome." Meg smiled. "We're still on for lunch after the holidays right? I can't wait to hear why Grantham and Margaret are headed to prison." She frowned. "And I really hope it has nothing to do with the scar on your forehead."

Priscilla chuckled and ran a finger along her scar. "Oh,

yeah. This has a *lot* to do with it.”

Meg was about to say something when Windy called out Priscilla’s name. Priscilla acknowledged her, then turned back to Meg. “I’ll leave my cell phone number with the Glenns tomorrow. Share it with Ashley and you ladies text me with a date that’ll work for the two of you.”

“Will do.” Meg motioned to her right. “Your friend is making her way through the crowd.”

“Oh, no. I’d better go. See you soon.” She grabbed the bag with Barry’s watch and walked toward Windy. “I told you I was on my way. Where’s Anthony’s mom? I’m looking forward to meeting her.”

“She’s still at the necklace counter. She’s found a couple of cross necklaces she wants to buy for Anthony and his brother. Ashley’s helping her. How did the rest of the conversation go with Meg?”

“Really well. Thank you for making me come. I was so afraid of what they’d thought of me, I don’t think I’d ever have come on my own.”

“You’re blessed to have a friend like me.”

Priscilla laughed. “I know.”

Windy winked. “I knew you’d agree.”

They stepped to the side as a young man was about to barrel through them. He stopped at the ring counter.

Windy scowled. “How rude.”

Priscilla shrugged. “Maybe he’s planning on proposing to someone on Christmas. That’ll explain his hurry to get a ring.”

“Or maybe he’s just a—”

“Windy.”

“Oh, my word. You sounded just like my sister when you said that.” She chuckled. “Come on, let’s head next door to the candle shop. This place is turning into a madhouse.”

“What about Anthony’s mom?”

“She’s already said she’s headed there next.” Windy turned in a circle. “I don’t see her anymore. She must’ve already left."

Priscilla waved goodbye to Meg and Ashley.

Thank you, Lord. Coming here today was not only a huge surprise and blessing, it also opened up the door for me to tell of Your Goodness to Ashley and Meg. Thank you for that opportunity. Go before me, Lord. Prepare their hearts and give me the words when the time comes.

The song, *O Come All Ye Faithful,* came through the speakers as they made their way through the crowd and toward the exit. Mama's favorite hymn.

Mama.

Priscilla stopped. "I should get Mama's Christmas gift while I'm here."

Windy pointed in the direction of the necklace display. "They have some beautiful gemstone necklaces over there. Miss Mabel likes sapphires, right?"

"She does, but Mama has so many necklaces. Gold, silver, pearl. She also has crosses with gemstones in them." Priscilla rubbed her chin. "She doesn't like to wear rings or bracelets. Earrings maybe?"

Windy shook her head. "That's something your sister would do. You're not Penelope. You're the wild child, remember? Give her something unexpected."

"Like what?"

"A toe ring. An ankle bracelet."

"What? Mama would kill me."

"Would she? How do you know? Does she have any?"

"No, but …"

"But what?"

"But, I don't know." Priscilla giggled. Now that she thought about it, Mama would only be surprised if the gift came from Penelope, but not her. She'd seen Priscilla in ankle bracelets before. Mama had never commented. She'd just frowned and shook her head. Yes, she'd totally expect Priscilla to give her a gift like that. "I can't believe I'm actually thinking about doing this."

Windy grabbed her hand and walked to a glass-enclosed case next to the rings. "They have some really nice ankle bracelets. She's gonna love it."

Priscilla let out a laugh so loud, several people turned and stared. She apologized and followed Windy's gaze.

Priscilla picked one out. She didn't know why Mama had always frowned upon ankle jewelry, and she also didn't know how Mama would respond to the gift. She'd probably hate it, but at least she'd get a good laugh out of Mama.

Or a slap.

Either way, it would be a Christmas to remember.

As the sales clerk wrapped the gift, she wondered if Chef Rigalta, or *Carlo*, as Mama called him, would be joining them for dinner this Christmas.

To her surprise, Priscilla hoped he would.

Chapter 27

Priscilla shoved the shopping bag hanging from her shoulder behind her and placed another one on the porch in front of the door. She and Windy had really outdone themselves. They had gone to at least ten different stores and two malls. Priscilla sighed. It was hard work, but at least she'd been able to scratch off everyone on her list.

Windy walked up the steps and set two larger shopping bags on the porch as well.

"You sure you don't want to ring the bell or call Barry for help?"

Priscilla maneuvered her purse in front of her and retrieved her keys. "No way. Barry's nosey and will snoop through the bags first chance he gets. And Mama's even worse."

Windy gave her a quick hug. "I'm getting out of this outfit before anyone else sees me." She jogged down the steps and turned back toward Windy. "See you later tonight."

A small local theater was having a classic movie marathon. Christianna, Liz, and Lola were going to meet them later that evening at the theater. Priscilla glanced at her watch. She had ninety-minutes to hide gifts and change clothes before she headed out again.

She giggled as a giddiness reminiscent of her childhood filled her. She couldn't wait to hang out with her friends again. Especially now, since there was no longer the threat of someone trying to kill her.

She'd also be out pretty late. The marathon ended at midnight, and she doubted they'd go their separate ways afterwards. More than likely, they'd end up at Windy's eating late night pizza. If Barry wasn't already home, she'd leave him a note. He'd started working from the main office again, and getting back into the swing of things. Priscilla could tell he enjoyed it. Barry was definitely one of those people who preferred doing business in a professional environment.

She waved as Windy drove off and jumped when she heard the door open behind her.

"Barry, you startled me. I wasn't sure if you were home yet."

"We have company."

The words came out through gritted teeth. His voice was low and his tone dry. Whoever the company was, it was apparent he didn't want them there.

"Is everything okay?"

He picked up several of the larger bags from the porch and she wrangled the others. When she and Windy had pulled into the driveway, there were no other cars. Barry more than likely had parked in the garage, but if they had company, their cars should've been in the driveway.

Unless they parked around the back, which was possible. But only family and close friends were allowed to do that. Mama always parked back there and so did Penelope, but she knew he wasn't referring to them. Barry would never refer to Mama or Penelope as *company*. Especially not in that tone.

One of her friends, maybe?

No. He liked her friends. All of them. He'd never react to a visit from them that way.

When they'd set her shopping bags down in the foyer, he turned to her. "Mabel called me at the office to let me know that Grantham and Victoria were here. They said they wanted to speak to you. They wouldn't tell Mabel why they wanted to see you, so she called me."

Grantham and Victoria wanted to see her? She groaned. The day had been going so well. The last thing she wanted to do was end it in an argument with her step-children.

"Did they tell *you* why they wanted to see me?"

He shook his head.

She placed his hand in hers. "Is that why you're so upset?"

"Grantham and I shared a few heated words. They're both in the hearth room. Do you want to talk to them?"

No, she didn't. "Curiosity is getting the best of me, but to be honest, Barry, I really don't."

He kissed her hand and walked down the hall that led to the hearth room.

"Where are you going?"

"To tell them to leave."

She hurried to catch up with him. "Don't. I'll see what they want. Just give me a minute to send a text to the girls. We were going to the movies tonight."

"You don't have to do this."

"I know, but I won't be able to sleep tonight if I don't."

He nodded. "I'll tell them."

"Thanks."

She pulled out her phone and sent a group text saying something urgent had come up and she wouldn't be able to make it. Liz immediately replied and asked if everything was all right. She typed a quick yes and invited everyone to come over the next afternoon. She didn't give a reason why, because she didn't have one. Well, she did, but she'd decided not to put it in a text. She just wanted to gather, have fun, and laugh with friends again.

Turns out she didn't need to give a reason. They'd all replied that they'd be there and share the info with Kite, Lydia, and Eve.

She inserted a 'thumbs up' emoji and slid the phone into her jeans pocket.

Lord, I don't know what Victoria and Grantham want to talk to me about. And I'm not even sure talking to them is a good idea, but I'm asking for Your help because I'm pretty sure I'm going to need it.

She blew out a breath and tossed her hair behind her shoulders. If she was going to get chewed out or threatened, she didn't want to look cute, she wanted to look *done*. Done with their sarcasm, snide remarks, and attitude. Done with their hate-filled eyes, threats, and intimidation.

Done with them.

She'd tried. She'd done everything she could to get them to accept her. Not just for Barry's sake, but for her own. She hated fighting with anyone, especially family. But she didn't start this fight.

They did.

She wasn't going to raise her voice or even engage in an argument. But she was going to let them know she was done with their antics. And if they didn't like it, then she was going to ask them to leave *her* house.

That would tick them off, but she no longer cared.

She lifted her chin. Time to end this nonsense once and for all.

She walked into the hearth room and was surprised to see Mama there, sitting in one of the upholstered recliners. She was even more surprised to see Chef Rigalta, *Carlo,* standing behind Mama's chair.

Barry stood in front of the corner bay window, arms folded across his chest.

Victoria sat on the hearth next to Grantham. Priscilla

read their faces. Victoria looked her in the eyes, but it wasn't an angry look. It almost looked as though she'd been crying. Was that even possible? To cry, you'd have to have a heart, and Priscilla wasn't convinced that Victoria had one.

Grantham didn't look at her. He'd slouched over when she'd entered the room, and he'd been focused on the floor ever since.

She glanced around the room again and smiled when her eyes met Barry's. They were his children, but he was there for her. Looking out for her, protecting her, supporting her. And so was Mama.

And *Carlo* was apparently there for her mother.

Hmph. Judging by the looks on their faces, none of them trusted Grantham and Victoria to be alone with Priscilla.

Victoria cleared her throat. "Dad, Mabel, Chef, would you mind giving us a minute alone with Priscilla?"

Mama scoffed. "I'm not going nowhere. State your business."

Victoria looked at Grantham, then turned back to Priscilla. "What we have to say may take a while. You might want to sit."

Priscilla folded her arms across her chest and widened her stance. Earlier, the three-inch heels worked against her as she tried to eavesdrop on Mama's and Chef's conversation. Now they worked for her.

Victoria was sitting, which made it easier for Priscilla to tower over her. The red boot color popped against her dark leggings and white sweater. She now wished she'd run upstairs and changed into her black sweater before talking to them. Black and red would've been the perfect combination for this conversation. She embraced her inner warrior, anyway. The red boots were meant to be festive and fun for her day out with Windy. Now she hoped they symbolized her rage. Victoria and Grantham had been harassing her for years. It ended today.

"Just get on with it."

Victoria lowered her eyes. "I'm not sure I know where to begin." She flicked her eyes to Priscilla. "That's not true. I need to start with an apology."

Victoria wiped at a bead of sweat that had made its way onto her forehead. She then wiped her hand against her tan corduroy pants.

"I still remember the day Dad told us about you. He'd shared how the two of you had met, the way you used to make a living, and what you looked like." She blew out a loud breath and closed her eyes. "It wasn't your past or your race that triggered my hatred of you. It was the way Dad *looked* when he talked about you. His eyes danced, and he smiled, and he even blushed a little. But that wasn't what burned a fire inside of me. It was the way he said your name. Not Priscilla, but the affectionate and soft way he called you Silly. There was so much love in that one stupid word that I immediately knew we were in trouble."

Grantham nodded.

Victoria continued, "Your past did raise a lot of questions, which is why we hired the investigators, but that wasn't what fueled our anger." She motioned toward Grantham with her thumb. "Dad's money, our inheritance, the estate… those were all Grantham's concerns. I was upset that Dad had decided to replace Mom."

Barry rubbed the back of his neck. Priscilla knew he was itching to say something and so was she. Priscilla let it go. She wanted to see where Victoria was headed. So far, she wasn't impressed. Sounded like the same old *blame everything on the new wife* game to her.

"Go on."

Victoria's eyes were still closed. "Mom died years ago, but I still mourn that loss." She shrugged. "A therapist once told me it was because I hadn't come to terms with the way we'd left things. Mom was heartbroken over the fact that Grantham and I had left the faith she'd spent so many years pouring into us." Tears rolled down her cheeks. "I remember being in this very room—it was their bedroom then—cuddling up with Grantham and Mom after Dad went to work. She'd read us one Bible story after the other. We'd ask questions, and she'd answer them. A lot of times, she'd have us act out the stories. My favorite was when Grantham played a king, I played David, and she acted out the part of Goliath.

"I can't speak for Grantham, but for me, as I got older, the whole God thing just didn't work for me anymore. I'd had the chance to travel abroad during my college years, and I'd seen too much pain and suffering to continue to believe in a just and loving God.

"I told Mom I'd walked away from the Christian faith in a phone call. Her silence told me how much that pained her. And whenever we'd get together after that, she'd want to discuss it. I wouldn't, she'd persist, and I'd end up storming out of the house. The last time I did that, she died two days later. I never got the chance to make it right or even say goodbye."

She reached behind her and pulled around a box of tissues. She yanked one from the box and blew her nose. "Years of therapy had gotten me to a place where I could function again, and I'd thought I was okay. But then Dad told us about you, and my world fell apart again.

"None of that excuses the way I treated you. Or how I hurt Dad. When I found out what Margaret and Grantham had done, I knew I couldn't do this anymore. I couldn't hang on to the bitterness and resentment like they did. They'd let it take them too far. Way too far. Margaret hired someone to kill you for crying out loud." She opened her eyes. "I never, *ever*, wanted anything like that to happen. I didn't like you, Priscilla, but I never wanted you dead. Please accept my apologies for any part I've played in this. I am so, so, sorry."

Priscilla walked over to Barry and sat in the leather chair next to him.

"I'm sorry, too." Grantham tossed his hands in the air.

"Victoria was right. It was all about Dad's money for me. Greed, plain and simple. It ate me up inside that you were going to inherit what I wanted the most—this property. And unfortunately, it wasn't because of the fond memories I've shared here with my family. It was the money."

He looked at Barry. "I don't know what happened to me, Dad. I don't. My obsession with your property and money … it was all I could think about." He turned to Priscilla. "Dad told me you know about my part in the hit-and-run and that I've been cleared of the attempted murder charges. Being cleared of those charges was important to me. Important enough for me to not try to protect my wife. I needed you, Dad, my sister, and my kids, to know that I'm not a murderer. I'm a lot of things, including a fool for hiring those goons to harass you in the first place, and for sharing that information with Margaret. I didn't hate you, Priscilla, and I don't now. I just wanted you out of Dad's life."

He chuckled and shook his head. "The love of money."

Victoria nodded. "Yep. Mom taught us about that, too."

"I know. I'm so glad she's not here to see the mess I've made of my life." He sniffed. "Priscilla, I'm sorry. For everything, including the scene I made in Prophet's. When the police showed me the footage, I was shocked. I didn't even recognize myself. I owe you more than an apology for that one. You name it, and I'll do it."

Priscilla thought about that for a second. Grantham definitely owed the employees at Prophet's an apology, but what did she want? What could Grantham—and Victoria too, for that matter—do to make up for all the pain they'd caused?

Nothing.

Barry stood behind her chair and massaged her shoulders. Grantham and Victoria weren't looking at her, but Mama and *Carlo* were.

The fact that Mama had referred to Chef that way earlier still bothered her. But it also reminded her of two things.

One, she and Victoria weren't that different. The loss of a parent had changed both of their lives. She'd lost Daddy, and Victoria had lost her mother. They'd both acted out. In different ways, sure, and even for different reasons, but with the same result—pain.

Pain and heartache for everyone who loved them.

Two, second chances. If God had shown her anything today, it was that everyone needed a second chance. In love and in life. God had given her a lot of second chances and had even thrown in boatloads of mercy to boot.

This wasn't fair. She'd come into this room prepared to fight. For her respect. Her dignity. Her peace of mind.

But there was a problem.

They hadn't come to her with swords. They'd come with repentant hearts.

Was God really asking her to give them another chance?

But she'd already given them so many.

Extend mercy?

After everything they'd done to her? To Barry?

Her mind flitted to a woman, bracing herself on dusty ground, waiting for the first stone.

She sucked in a breath. When she didn't release it, Barry shook her shoulder. "You okay?"

She nodded. "Grantham, you asked me to name anything and you'd do it. Did you really mean that?"

"Yes."

"Victoria, what about you? Do you feel the same way?"

"Absolutely. Whatever it is, I'll do it."

"Good. Because I don't want you to do anything." Priscilla stood. "I want to give you something."

They narrowed their eyes and looked behind her to Barry. She didn't know what kind of look their dad gave them, but they both stood.

Grantham shoved his hands in his pockets. "What do you want to give us?"

"If you don't mind," Priscilla choked back tears. "I'd

like to give you both a hug."

Priscilla took a step forward but was almost knocked back into her chair from the force of Grantham and Victoria running to her. Victoria wrapped her arms around Priscilla's middle and Grantham hugged her from the side. Barry's hand supported her back.

Victoria sobbed in her ear. "Please forgive me."

Priscilla ran her fingers through Victoria's hair, just like Mama had always done with her when she was upset.

"All is forgiven."

Grantham hugged her tighter. "I'm sorry for all the awful things I've said to you. I'm a terrible person. I'm—"

"Loved."

He pulled away from her. "What?"

"You're loved."

His eyes watered. "By who? My wife hates me. Dad'll never trust me again. Victoria's disgusted with me. I hired men to harrass you. Who's left to love me?"

"God."

He stared at her before curling his lips into a smile. "He must love me, because He's put someone in my life who talks about Him the same way my mom did. Maybe this time, I'll get it right."

Victoria kissed her brother on the forehead. "You know I love you."

Barry wrapped his arms around the three of them. Priscilla blinked away more tears. She needed to stop all this crying before Mama …

She lifted her head toward where Mama was sitting. Mama's head was on Carlo's shoulder, and she was wiping away her own tears.

Priscilla chuckled. Could this day hold any more surprises?

Chapter 28

Priscilla held Rich Brown's reins in her hands and tried to remember everything Francine said to her that morning.

Before they went to bed last night, she and Barry watched the weather forecast. When the meteorologist said the morning forecast was going to be sunny and in the mid-sixties—odd for a November day in Missouri—she knew it'd be the perfect opportunity for her to train on Rich Brown again.

Francine had made sure Rich Brown stayed active during Priscilla's recovery. For a while, Priscilla had been able to go into the barn to groom him and give him treats, but all that stopped the day the stable hands found Pharaoh Kaador in the woods.

But all of that was behind her now. With the exception of Grantham, everyone involved in her *accident* had been apprehended and jailed, though it was only a matter of time before he joined them. Before yesterday, she'd looked forward to seeing him behind bars.

Not so much today.

Yesterday, they were a family. And she'd enjoyed every minute of it. After everyone had stopped hugging and crying, Mama and Carlo had made their way to the kitchen and whipped up a Chinese dinner so delicious, Priscilla was sure it would've made every Asian restaurant in Habakkuk jealous.

Afterward, Grantham's lawyer stopped by to talk about his case. Barry told them they could use his home office. Grantham asked his dad to join them. His lawyer scoffed at that idea and said absolutely not. When Barry said he was no longer interested in pressing charges against Grantham, the lawyer relented, and the three of them stayed in Barry's office for hours.

Mama, Victoria, and Priscilla chatted at the kitchen table. Mama shared with Victoria some of her favorite memories with Edith, and Chef made sure they had plenty of homemade boba ice cream.

Priscilla no longer had to guess if there was something between Chef and Mama. The way they'd continued to interact with each other had removed all doubt.

She'd pushed Mama for answers, but all Mama would say was that they were companions. Priscilla had asked what exactly she'd meant by that, but Mama said she'd said enough. Priscilla thought about asking Chef directly, but quickly nixed that idea. He was still her employee, and she didn't want their professional relationship turning awkward.

Mama disappeared with Victoria after that. Priscilla suspected Mama had taken Victoria aside to talk to her about the dangers of trying to communicate with the dead.

"Mrs. King, I *really* need you to pay attention."

Priscilla tightened her grip on the reins. "I'm sorry, Francine. My mind got away from me for a minute. I'm listening now."

"Rich Brown's a pretty tame horse, but he's still a horse. Not paying attention can end up with someone getting hurt."

Priscilla stiffened. She didn't like being chastised by

someone young enough to be her daughter. She lowered her chin to her chest. But... Francine was right. She was probably only in her late-twenties, but she'd been around horses her whole life. Priscilla hadn't. She needed to swallow her pride and listen to the person who actually knew what she was doing.

Francine reached up and loosened Priscilla's grip on the reins. She then helped Priscilla straighten her back.

Francine said, "I'm now going to lead him into a trot around the arena. Remember, I need you to round your hips and pay attention to his footfall. Why is that important?"

Priscilla chewed her lip and thought back to Francine's words from earlier this morning. "Because I need to be in rhythm with the horse?"

Francine chuckled. "That's not exactly what I said, but it is one of the reasons, so I'll accept that. Ready?"

Priscilla nodded and focused on her balance. She wanted to just relax and enjoy the ride, but Francine had told her many times before that she would only be able to do that *after* she'd learned the basics. And one of the things Francine constantly had to correct her on was her balance.

After several successful laps around the arena, Priscilla spotted Barry watching them. He was smiling. Priscilla returned the smile and relaxed a bit more. So far, she'd only had one correction from Francine, and that was a huge improvement.

When Francine saw Barry, she brought Rich Brown to a halt. "That was really good, Mrs. King. I'm impressed."

"Thank you." Priscilla glanced at her watch. She still had about an hour before her friends arrived. "I have time to go around a couple of more times, if you don't mind."

Francine nodded toward Barry. "We could if you want, but I'm not sure how productive that would be."

Priscilla frowned. "What do you mean?"

Francine kicked at a clump of dirt. When she looked up, she was smiling.

"When Mr. King is around, you're a lot harder to work with. Easily distracted."

Priscilla looked at Barry, who'd already made his way into the arena. He was tanned, fit, and had a way of looking at her that put all sorts of crazy thoughts into her head. How could she *not* be distracted?

She placed a gloved hand over her face. "I'm so embarrassed."

Francine chuckled. "For what? He's the love of your life. You're allowed to be distracted. If the weather holds out, we can just pick up tomorrow."

Barry appeared at her side and lifted her off the horse. His lips were on hers before her feet hit the ground.

She vaguely heard Francine mention something about taking Rich Brown to the barn.

Barry held her tight against him. "Good job. You've improved a lot. You'll be riding with me on the trails in no time."

"No thanks to you." Priscilla teased. "I would've been able to get more training in if you hadn't shown up. Francine says I'm easily distracted when you're around."

"I know." He loosened his hold. "She's mentioned that to me before, which is why I try to stay away when she's teaching you."

"You never told me she said that."

He shrugged. "I didn't want you to get mad at her. I know how much you love having me around."

"You do, do you?"

"Oh, yeah. You can't help yourself. You're madly in love with me."

"I am, am I?"

"See? You can't even form complete sentences when I'm around. I take your thoughts *and* your breath away."

Priscilla laughed and threw herself back into his arms. "Kiss me again."

He smiled. "I'd love to, but there's a reason I came to

distract you. We have company."

She looked at her watch. It was almost noon. "Already? I thought I had more time."

"Lydia's here and so is Eve." He cleared his throat. "I don't know how to tell you this, so I'll just say it straight out—your mom has stolen your friends."

She laughed again as they made their way toward the house. "I'm not surprised. It's like high school all over again. My friends would come to see me, then end up talking and hanging out with Mama."

"She does have a way about her that draws people in."

"I know." They climbed the steps to the back porch. When Barry pulled the screen door open, voices filled the air. Priscilla easily recognized Windy's. She must've arrived while Barry was in the arena.

When they stepped inside, Lydia walked up to her. "There you are. Mabel filled us in on everything that happened yesterday. I'm so glad things are working out between you, Grantham, and Victoria."

"It was totally unexpected. When Barry and I married, we knew it would be difficult for them, but it wasn't until yesterday that we understood why. Thank you for your prayers. I know you spent many hours on your knees with Mama. You have no idea how much we appreciate that."

"It's what I've been called to do."

Windy, Kite, Eve, and Christianna joined them. A few minutes later, Shields entered the kitchen with Liz.

Windy furrowed her brows and motioned toward Shields. "Who's that guy with Liz?"

"One of our stable hands. His name is Shields Canaan. He's also Liz's fiancé."

Windy's eyes widened.

Kite's lips parted.

Lydia smiled.

Eve placed her hands over her heart.

Christianna stared at Shields. After a few moments, she

pointed at him and shouted, "The Habakkuk Lions. That's where I know you from."

Everyone laughed at Christianna's outburst, but Priscilla was laughing for a different reason. Like the rest of her friends, she'd known Christianna since childhood. She wasn't surprised that Christianna voiced her thoughts out loud because that was typical behavior for her. She was laughing, because like Priscilla, Christianna had an older sister. And just like Penelope would chastise Priscilla for being uncouth, Christianna's sister Mary would do the same to her younger sibling. Priscilla could only imagine the *look* Mary would give her little sister now.

Liz walked over and showed everyone her ring. She then apologized for keeping her upcoming nuptials a secret and gave a brief explanation as to why. She even answered the dreaded, *does he know about your past* question.

She assured them she'd told Shields everything, and Priscilla couldn't have been prouder of her friend. She knew how hard sharing that information with her fiancé had to have been for her.

Ram and Lola arrived, and Liz ran over to them. Lola let out a *"I knew it"* scream a moment later. Lola had been the first one to say that Shields and Liz were made for each other.

Priscilla looked around. She'd had Chef and Mama set out every ingredient possible for her and the girls to make Christmas cookies.

There were candies, sprinkles, various sugars, and flours in glass bowls along the quartz counter. There were also four mixers with sticks of butter next to each.

Priscilla had thought it'd be a fun way for them to jumpstart the Christmas season, but as she glanced around the room, she knew it wasn't her only reason.

She'd needed this. She'd needed her friends, their laughter, and the joy and lightheartedness that tagged along with them.

And the freedom.

She closed her eyes, sucked in a deep breath, and embraced it.

There was nothing new about gathering with her friends and having a good time. They'd done it many times over the years.

But this was the first time she was *free* to enjoy the good times with them.

They'd never made her feel like stones were about to be thrown her way—she did.

Back then, images from her past would bombard and taunt her, and she'd feel dirty and out of place.

But not today.

Or ever again.

It had taken a long time, and the journey had been rough, but she now understood what God had been trying to tell her all along.

Whom the Son sets free, is free indeed.

She didn't know exactly when her heart had completely understood that truth, but it had.

And she never planned on forgetting it.

-------THE END-------

Kara R. Hunt enjoys both fiction and non-fiction and has been a contributing author to the devotional, Marriage Matters. Kara, an evangelical minister, hosts the Cheer UP! Podcast. She is a member of the Advanced Writers and Speakers Association (AWSA), Faith, Hope, & Love Christian Writers (FHLCW), and American Christian Fiction Writers. She has garnered finalist and semi-finalist recognition in the ACFW Genesis Awards in the Mystery/Thriller/Suspense and Women's Fiction categories. Kara and her husband reside in rural Missouri.

SOCIAL MEDIA LINKS

Website: https://kararhunt.com/

Goodreads: https://www.goodreads.com/user/show/2610898-kara-r-hunt

Author Facebook: https://www.facebook.com/AuthorKaraRHunt

Instagram: https://www.instagram.com/kararhunt/

Twitter: https://twitter.com/KaraRHunt2022

Pinterest:
https://www.pinterest.com/AuthorKaraRHunt/_save
d/

Linked: https://www.linkedin.com/in/kara-hunt-
23b4a1220/

Book 1 / Paper Dolls -
https://www.amazon.com/dp/B09S3W9K1W

Book 2 / Kite: Paper Dolls
https://www.amazon.com/Kite-Paper-Dolls-Habakkuk-
Book-ebook/dp/B0BDZVW4SW

www.ingramcontent.com/pod-product-compliance
Lightning Source LLC
Chambersburg PA
CBHW070457200726
48293CB00007B/2254